Marsh Henderson looked even more dangerously handsome in the light of day than he had in the dark of night.

And she would bet he could tempt a post-menopausal nun to sin with one of his devastating grins if he put his mind to it. In fact, her skin prickled whenever he so much as cranked up a smile.

But she'd darn well better remember he was here to lure another man into a trap, and she was here as bait. Her only purpose in accompanying Marsh to this mountain retreat was to protect her sister.

She would remind herself of that sobering fact every time her skin started to prickle.

D1025715

Dear Reader,

It's time to go wild with Intimate Moments. First, welcome historical star Ruth Langan back to contemporary times as she begins her new family-oriented trilogy. *The Wildes of Wyoming—Chance* is a slam-bang beginning that will leave you eager for the rest of the books in the miniseries. Then look for *Wild Ways,* the latest in Naomi Horton's WILD HEARTS miniseries. The first book, *Wild Blood,* won a Romance Writers of America RITA Award for this talented author, and this book is every bit as terrific.

Stick around for the rest of our fabulous lineup, too. Merline Lovelace continues MEN OF THE BAR H with *Mistaken Identity,* full of suspense mixed with passion in that special recipe only Merline seems to know. Margaret Watson returns with *Family on the Run,* the story of a sham marriage that awakens surprisingly real emotions. Maggie Price's *On Dangerous Ground* is a MEN IN BLUE title, and this book has a twist that will leave you breathless. Finally, welcome new author Nina Bruhns, whose dream of becoming a writer comes true this month with the publication of her first book, *Catch Me If You Can.*

You won't want to miss a single page of excitement as only Intimate Moments can create it. And, of course, be sure to come back next month, when the passion and adventure continue in Silhouette Intimate Moments, where excitement and romance go hand in hand.

Enjoy!

Leslie J. Wainger
Executive Senior Editor

Please address questions and book requests to:
Silhouette Reader Service
U.S.: 3010 Walden Ave., P.O. Box 1325, Buffalo, NY 14269
Canadian: P.O. Box 609, Fort Erie, Ont. L2A 5X3

MISTAKEN IDENTITY
MERLINE LOVELACE

Published by Silhouette Books
America's Publisher of Contemporary Romance

If you purchased this book without a cover you should be aware
that this book is stolen property. It was reported as "unsold and
destroyed" to the publisher, and neither the author nor the
publisher has received any payment for this "stripped book."

To my dad, who reads every one of my books—
thanks for gifting me with your love of adventure and
joy in books!

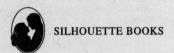 SILHOUETTE BOOKS

ISBN 0-373-07987-7

MISTAKEN IDENTITY

Copyright © 2000 by Merline Lovelace

All rights reserved. Except for use in any review, the reproduction
or utilization of this work in whole or in part in any form by any
electronic, mechanical or other means, now known or hereafter
invented, including xerography, photocopying and recording, or in
any information storage or retrieval system, is forbidden without
the written permission of the editorial office, Silhouette Books,
300 East 42nd Street, New York, NY 10017 U.S.A.

All characters in this book have no existence outside the imagination of
the author and have no relation whatsoever to anyone bearing the same
name or names. They are not even distantly inspired by any individual
known or unknown to the author, and all incidents are pure invention.

This edition published by arrangement with Harlequin Books S.A.

® and TM are trademarks of Harlequin Books S.A., used under license.
Trademarks indicated with ® are registered in the United States Patent
and Trademark Office, the Canadian Trade Marks Office and in other
countries.

Visit us at www.romance.net

Printed in U.S.A.

MERLINE LOVELACE

spent twenty-three exciting years as an air force officer, serving tours at the Pentagon and at bases all over the world before she began a new career as a novelist. When she's not tied to her keyboard, she and her own handsome hero, Al, enjoy traveling, golf and long, lively dinners with friends and family.

Look for her next book, *The Harder They Fall,* the fourth in her sexy MEN OF THE BAR H series, coming in April from Silhouette Intimate Moments.

Merline enjoys hearing from readers and can be reached at P.O. Box 892717, Oklahoma City, OK, 73189, or by e-mail via Harlequin's web site at http://www.romance.net

IT'S OUR 20th ANNIVERSARY!
We'll be celebrating all year, continuing with these fabulous titles, on sale in February 2000.

Special Edition

#1303 Man...Mercenary... Monarch
Joan Elliott Pickart

#1304 Dr. Mom and the Millionaire
Christine Flynn

#1305 Who's That Baby?
Diana Whitney

#1306 Cattleman's Courtship
Lois Faye Dyer

#1307 The Marriage Basket
Sharon De Vita

#1308 Falling for an Older Man
Trisha Alexander

Intimate Moments

#985 The Wildes of Wyoming—Chance
Ruth Langan

#986 Wild Ways
Naomi Horton

#987 Mistaken Identity
Merline Lovelace

#988 Family on the Run
Margaret Watson

#989 On Dangerous Ground
Maggie Price

#990 Catch Me If You Can
Nina Bruhns

Romance

 VIRGIN BRIDES
#1426 Waiting for the Wedding
Carla Cassidy

#1427 Bringing Up Babies
Susan Meier

#1428 The Family Diamond
Moyra Tarling

#1429 Simon Says...Marry Me!
Myrna Mackenzie

#1430 The Double Heart Ranch
Leanna Wilson

#1431 If the Ring Fits...
Melissa McClone

Desire

#1273 A Bride for Jackson Powers
Dixie Browning

#1274 Sheikh's Temptation
Alexandra Sellers

#1275 The Daddy Salute
Maureen Child

#1276 Husband for Keeps
Kate Little

#1277 The Magnificent M.D.
Carol Grace

#1278 Jesse Hawk: Brave Father
Sheri WhiteFeather

Prologue

Marsh Henderson leaned his shoulders against a lodgepole pine support beam, tipped his black Stetson lower over his eyes, and squinted through the dying rays of the northern Arizona sun.

In the distance, a blazing sunset flamed the snow-capped San Francisco Peaks to a bright gold. In closer, paper lanterns strung around the flagstone patio offered their own riot of color. The snappy strains of a two-step danced across the late August air that carried a hint of the fall that came early at these elevations.

Lord, it felt good to be back at the Bar-H. Marsh wasn't sure until the last minute whether he'd be able to steal away to join the festivities welcoming the newest addition to the Henderson clan. The mo-

ment he'd turned his Blazer onto the dusty road to
the ranch, he'd felt the tension that came with his
job ease.

Here in the shadow of the rugged San Franciscos,
listening to the laughter of his friends and family,
he could almost forget the stack of reports waiting
for him in El Paso. Could almost blank out the grim
images of the massacre perpetrated by the Drug Enforcement Administration's newest #1 fugitive, still
at large somewhere in Marsh's district.

Why the hell had he ever gone into law enforcement? he wondered, not for the first time. Why had
he traded the blue skies and high-mountain air of
Bar-H for the dark underworld of drug dealers and
acid heads? Big John had wanted him to stay home
and help run the spread—had wanted all five of his
boys to stay.

The rowdy young Hendersons had been too ram-
bunctious to remain at home, and too eager to ex-
plore the world outside of Arizona. They'd all left—
for school, for military service, for the careers that
took them to every corner of the globe. But they all
came back every chance they got—to help bring the
summer-fattened herds down from the high pastures
in autumn, to wrestle bawling new calves into chutes
during the spring roundup, and to gather for wed-
dings and christenings and funerals.

Only Jake, the oldest, had returned for good after
his hitch in the Marines, first working for his father,
and then, after Big John's death, running the Bar-H
along with his own spread. Of course, he'd had good

reason to dig his boot heels into the rich volcanic soil of northern Arizona. Brawny, hard-headed Jake had been in love with shy, elfin Ellen for as long as any of the Hendersons could remember.

Jake had been the first of the five brothers to bite the matrimonial dust. Sam, the youngest, went next. Then, surprising everyone, Reece. Now only Marsh and Evan retained their free and easy bachelor ways…although hanging on to their freedom was getting harder to do in the face of the persistent efforts by their various sisters-in-law.

Like Sydney.

Marsh swallowed a groan as he spotted Reece's bride of seven months making her way across the patio, another potential candidate in tow. Sydney had brought a film crew to the Bar-H to shoot both the ancient Anasazi ruins around Flagstaff, twenty miles away, and the festivities to welcome Kasey Duncan Henderson, Sam and Molly's gurgling addition to the clan. Syd must have scoured L.A. to come up with every single, divorced, or otherwise unattached female camera operator or sound manager. This one wasn't bad, Marsh conceded, if your tastes ran to rail-thin blondes with size-sixteen egos poured into size-four jeans.

"Hey, Marsh."

"Hey, yourself, Syd."

"My husband claims you're the only Henderson who doesn't trip over his own feet on a dance floor."

"Your husband knows whereof he speaks. Want to take a turn?"

"I can't. I'm next in line to hold Kasey so Molly and Sam can chow down. But I went to a few L.A. discos with Andrea here before Reece turned me into an stodgy old married woman. Trust me, she can make every move known to man."

Somehow, that didn't surprise Marsh. But because he genuinely liked the vibrant, dark-haired dynamo who'd battled a raging river and a crumbling hydro-electric dam alongside his brother, he didn't say so. Good-naturedly, he tipped his hat to the blonde.

"Care to show me a few of those moves, Andrea?"

"Whenever you're ready, cowboy."

Feeling smug with the results of her matchmaking, Sydney watched Marsh lead the scriptwriter to the flagstone patio. Viewing his tall, broad-shouldered frame against the last rays of the dying sun made her fingers itch for a camera. Like all the Hendersons, Marsh possessed a rugged handsomeness that could stop a girl's breath at twenty paces and the long-legged swagger of a man who didn't have to ask for much in this world.

"You're wasting your time."

Sydney turned at the sound of a soft voice. Ellen, the most senior and the shiest of the three Henderson brides, had known the brothers all her life.

"Marsh is as stubborn as Evan when it comes to hanging on to his bachelor ways."

"They can't hold out forever," Sydney replied

with cheerful ruthlessness. "If they're going to fall, I'd just as soon they fall for someone I know and like."

Ellen's laughter rippled above the music. "Jake says the snowcaps on the San Franciscos will melt before Evan does. He's got his life arranged just the way he likes it."

"So I've noticed," the younger woman grumbled, recalling the string of friends and associates she'd already paraded past the rakishly handsome assistant D.A. "So what's Marsh's excuse? He doesn't have any routine at all that I can see. Half the time he's under cover. The other half, he's on the street dodging bullets."

The laughter in Ellen's dove-gray eyes dimmed. "That's the problem. The one and only time Marsh fell in love, his fiancée came apart at the seams when he took a bullet in the chest. She broke off their engagement while he was still in ICU."

"Oh, nice!" Sydney's gaze went to the tall, broad-shouldered DEA agent. "When did that happen?"

"About four years ago."

"Someone should have told me."

The laughter crept back into Ellen's eyes. "I wanted to, but Jake said not to spoil the fun. He and the others get such a kick out of watching you put Marsh through his paces."

Her sunny smile back in full force now, Ellen looped her arm through her sister-in-law's. "Come on, let's go steal the baby from Molly. I've hardly had any cuddle time yet."

Sydney went with her, casting a last look at the couple moving with languid grace around the roped-off dance area. Marsh gave every indication of enjoying the partner who'd just stopped short of wrapping herself around him, but Sydney knew him well enough now to recognize the signs. His hormones were engaged, but not his interest.

So much for Andrea.

She refused to let another strike-out discourage her. Maybe she'd invite Marissa Parks to join them the next time the Hendersons got together. Surely the dazzlingly beautiful, up-and-coming young actress could generate some sparks.

Happily unaware of his sister-in-law's plans, Marsh managed to shed his clinging partner after two dances and joined his brothers at the tin washtub filled with melting ice and Coors. He popped a top, and let the beer go down cold and fast.

"Steering Sydney's friend around the patio hard work?" Evan ribbed.

"Why don't you try it and find out?"

"No, thanks. I did my duty by the flirty little cousin she sicced on me last month."

Dismissing his older brother with a grunt, Marsh appealed to Reece. "What's the odds of your wife running out of candidates any time soon?"

"Pretty slim," the ex-bachelor stated with a grin. "She's got more friends and connections than we have wide-open spaces here at the Bar-H."

Since the spread that Big John Henderson had carved out of the northern Arizona plateau ran to some twenty thousand acres, with grazing rights to ten thousand more in the Coconino Forest, that bit of information afforded neither Evan nor Marsh much relief. It did, however, lead to a change in subject. The four younger Hendersons may have left the ranch to pursue other professions, but the ranch had never left them. Within moments, they were deep in discussion about Jake's proposed purchase of a new bull.

While his brothers argued the relative merits of Charolais and British Red Poll, Marsh swept the patio with another glance. This was the Bar-H as he always remembered it. The San Franciscos looming to the east. The spectacular sunsets. The Hendersons talking cattle and grazing rights.

He'd have to get home more often, he decided. Visit with Jake and Ellen. Ride the hills. He always let too many months slide by between visits, got too caught up in the dark underworld of counter narcotics. With that promise hanging lazy in his mind, he took another pull on his beer.

Marsh left the Bar-H the next morning. He returned exactly two weeks later, only hours after being jerked from sleep by the shrilling phone…and by the brutal news that Ellen had just been killed in a drive-by shooting in Phoenix, on her way to visit her college roommate.

Chapter 1

After almost thirty-six hours of continuous surveillance, Marsh caught the sound of a car pulling up in front of the house next door.

Every one of his senses jumped to full alert. Moving like a silent shadow through the darkened living room, he flattened himself against the wall and lifted the blinds an inch. When he saw the unmistakable silhouette of a woman climb out of a taxi, his heart picked up speed.

It was her! Rebecca Smith. It had to be. The hair was longer than in the picture on her Arizona driver's license, but even in the dim glow of the streetlights Marsh couldn't miss its gleaming auburn tints. Just to make sure, he grabbed the night-vision binoculars he'd appropriated for this stakeout.

"Come on," he urged, his gaze drilling into the woman's back. "Turn around. Let me have a look at you."

Marsh gripped the binoculars and stared unblinking through sandpapery eyes at the image haloed in the greenish glow. He'd hardly slept or eaten since that grim night when Reece had relayed the gut-wrenching news of Ellen's death that had brought the Hendersons back to the Bar-H once again.

Marsh knew he'd never wipe that gray, drizzly day of the funeral from his mind. He, Reece, Sam and Evan had been pallbearers, while Jake stood stony-eyed and silent. With his mother on one side, and his sisters-in-law on the other, the eldest of the Henderson brothers had watched as his wife was lowered into an earth just browning after the first touches of frost.

They'd stayed with Jake as long as they could, but knew that the loss wouldn't really hit him until everyone left and he was alone with his memories of Ellen. Their mother was still at the Bar-H, in the house she'd come to as a bride and had left after Big John died. Jessica Henderson intended to remain with her son until they both came to grips with Ellen's senseless, tragic death.

Except it wasn't senseless. It was a brutal, if misdirected, murder. And Marsh was going to bring the man behind the shooting to justice.

Long weeks of determined investigation, dogged persistence and ruthless shaking down of every snitch in southern Arizona had finally paid off. Ten days ago, the Phoenix police had busted a small-time crack dealer. In an attempt to beat the rap, the doper let drop that he'd witnessed the incident that had made all the Phoenix papers.

The dealer also confirmed that the drive-by shooting was no random act. Another car sped through the intersection at the precise moment the shots were fired. The driver of that car was the intended target, the police informed Marsh. Ellen just happened to get in the way.

The doper's description of the other vehicle led to an ID of the owner—one David Jannisek—a Phoenix hotelier with a weakness for fast redheads and not-so-fast horses. Allegedly, Jannisek owed hundreds of thousands to the mob boss rumored to control the southwest. But before the police could close in on him, he'd disappeared.

The investigators had then set their sights on the flamboyant hotelier's latest love…the cocktail waitress who, according to all reports, Jannisek had fallen for in a big way, and for whom he had dug himself even deeper into debt. The police figured she might lead them to her missing lover, who in turn could finger the man behind the attempt on his life. When they'd interviewed her, however, Jannisek's companion had denied all knowledge of either the shooting or her boyfriend's whereabouts. Just days ago she, like Jannisek, had disappeared.

With all leads played out and nowhere else to look, the overworked homicide detectives had been forced to put the case on the back burner. A grimly determined Marsh had picked up where they'd left off. After informing his boss that he was taking an unpaid leave of absence, he'd jumped onto the next plane leaving El Paso for Phoenix.

The locals had cooperated as much as they could. They'd brought him up to speed on the investigation to date and turned over copies of their case files. They'd even arranged a walk through the missing woman's rented house. One glance at the disarray inside told Marsh she'd left in a hell of a hurry…and that she'd return sooner or later to reclaim her possessions. Assuming she was still alive.

Al Ramos, the detective in charge of the case, believed both Jannisek and his girlfriend had disappeared for good. Maybe the mob had tried again after the first botched shooting that had taken Ellen's life. Maybe they'd find the bodies of both the handsome hotelier and his girlfriend in an arroyo one of these days.

Marsh refused to settle for ''maybe's.'' None of the sources the police had shaken down could say with any certainty that Jannisek had been taken out. Unless or until he and/or Becky Smith turned up dead, they constituted the only lead to the shadowy figure responsible for Ellen's death. Grimly determined, Marsh had rented the house next door to Smith, hunkered down, and spent thirty-six long, empty hours waiting for the target to show.

Now it looked as though his wait might just have paid off.

His jaw tight, he adjusted the focus on the high-powered binoculars. He forgot to breathe, forgot everything until the woman finished paying the cabbie, slung her oversized tote bag over her shoulder, and turned. Her face blurred, and then filled the lenses.

"Bingo," Marsh said, softly.

With the keen eye of a hunter, he cataloged his prey's features. Full, sensuous mouth. High cheeks. Eyes wide-spaced under winged black brows. Wine-colored hair parted just off center and falling in sleek folds to her shoulders.

What clinched her identity for Marsh, however, was the pin on the lapel of her caramel-colored linen jacket. Even from this distance, he couldn't mistake the wink of diamonds as she hurried up the walk. Eyes narrowed, he adjusted the focus to zero in on the fanciful little unicorn brooch.

Triumph brought a savage smile to Marsh's face. He recognized that pin. He'd seen a picture of it in the case file. A laughing Becky Smith had purchased the expensive piece just weeks ago and airily instructed the clerk to charge it to David Jannisek's account. The store clerk had described the pin in detail to the detectives trying to track down Jannisek. He'd described the luscious Ms. Smith in some detail, too.

Marsh had to admit the clerk hadn't missed the mark. Becky Smith was a looker. Her face appeared more fine-boned in the flesh than in the photo on her three-year-old driver's license. What hadn't shown in the photo were her killer body and the mile-long legs that gave Marsh an unexpected kick to the stomach.

The gut-level reaction annoyed the hell out of him. Of course she would come equipped with supple curves and a mouth made for sin. She'd have to pack something extraordinary to keep a playboy like Jannisek dancing to her tune…along with the half dozen other men who'd enjoyed Becky Smith's companionship at various times in her short, busy career as a cocktail waitress.

Blanking his mind to the body displayed to perfection by tight jeans, a black stretchy top and the hip-skimming linen jacket, Marsh waited with mounting anticipation for her to climb the few steps to the front stoop.

She went up the shallow stairs, reached for the door, froze.

"That's right, sweetheart." Wire-tight with tension, he kept the binoculars on her profile. "The door's open. Make you nervous?"

She hesitated, indecision in every line of her body. Interminable seconds ticked by. Marsh held his breath, willing her to take the next step. Finally, she gave the door a tentative push. It swung wide open, revealing nothing but blackness inside the small stucco house.

"Go inside," he urged fiercely. "Come on, you know you want to."

His prey hovered on the stoop. Any woman with half a lick of common sense would turn around and run to the nearest house with lights on to call the police. Marsh was counting on the fact that Rebecca Smith would do exactly the opposite. Every bit of information he'd gathered on the fickle, flirtatious Becky indicated she was better known for her kittenish sensuality than her common sense.

After endless seconds of indecision, she stepped into the darkness. The lights inside the house flicked on, spilling a bright glow into the night. A moment later, the front door slammed shut.

Savage satisfaction coursed through Marsh's veins. Phase One was under way.

Dropping the binoculars, he checked his watch. Five minutes—he'd give her five minutes before he implemented the next phase of his plan to trap Ellen's killer.

His pulse hammering, Marsh leaned against the wall. It didn't bother him in the least that he was operating outside the parameters of his authority, and with only the tacit consent of the locals. Or that the detective in charge of the case had clearly considered staking out Rebecca Smith's house a waste of time.

Marsh had been a cop long enough to trust his instincts, and his walk through the house next door had convinced him Smith would come back. She might be the world's sexiest waitress. She certainly qualified as the world's worst housekeeper. But she also, Marsh discovered during his search, had expensive tastes. Very expensive. A woman who collected diamond jewelry and undies of the Neiman-

Marcus variety wasn't going to leave them all behind.

With a grunt, Marsh fought to banish the erotic image that jumped into his mind. He had no business imagining the woman he'd just pinned in the binoculars in a pair of those skimpy, lace-trimmed thong panties. Her long legs and rounded hips would certainly do them justice, though. No wonder Jannisek had gone off the deep end and lost more at the track than he could ever hope to pay back, in an attempt to impress Rebecca Smith.

The gambler's unpaid debts had come close to getting him killed, Marsh remembered, with a twist of his gut. Instead, Ellen had taken the bullets meant for Jannisek.

He flicked another impatient glance at his watch.

Three minutes to Phase Two.

His blood racing with anticipation, he closed his eyes and focused his thoughts on the woman next door. The open front door would have shaken her. She'd be scared now, and with good reason. In three minutes, Marsh intended to frighten her even more.

Her nerves jumping like live electrical wires, Lauren Smith stood amid the shambles of her sister's bedroom. Discarded clothes lay everywhere. Glossy fashion magazines were scattered across the floor and the unmade bed. An empty pizza carton occupied the chair by the window. The stuffed and porcelain Garfields Becky collected grinned down gleefully at the mess.

Was anything missing? Had the place been burgled? For the life of her, Lauren couldn't tell.

Becky thrived on chaos. In her home. In her work. In her life. With a mere ten months separating the sisters, it had always amazed Lauren that they could look almost like twins, yet possess such diametrically opposite personalities. The laughing, irrepressible Becky flitted through life as though it were one huge game to be played to the fullest. Cautious, careful Lauren had always followed more slowly, often cleaning up the messes Becky left in her wake.

Like this one.

"What the heck have you gotten yourself into this time?" she murmured, as she had repeatedly since she'd returned to Denver from a trip to D.C.'s National Gallery of Art earlier this afternoon. She'd hit the button on her phone recorder, and heard her sister's voice leap out at her.

Something had happened, Becky had exclaimed. She...she needed to take some time to think things through and decide what to do. Call me, she had demanded. A second message the next day had expressed impatience that Lauren wasn't home, and then cut off abruptly then in Becky's usual haphazard style.

Lauren had called immediately, only to listen in frustration to the endless ringing. All afternoon she'd redialed, wondering and worrying.

What had happened? What did Becky need to think through? Even more disturbing, what had put an uncharacteristic tremor in her sister's voice?

Lauren's worry had mounted with each unanswered phone call. After hours of pacing and dialing, she did what the sisters had always done in a crisis—rush to the other's aid. With just moments to spare, she caught the seven-ten flight out of Denver for Phoenix.

Now that she was here, though, she didn't have a clue what to do next. Where was her sister? Had she skipped town, or merely gone out for the evening?

Chewing on her lower lip, Lauren skimmed another glance at the unmade bed, the clothes tossed carelessly on the floor, the Garfield cats decorating the old-fashioned vanity with its oval mirror, a relic right out of the 30s that the perpetually broke Becky had found in a junk shop and beautifully restored.

That was Becky, Lauren reflected, her mouth curving. On paydays she'd splurge on a leg wax or the expensive lingerie she collected with as much passion as her Garfield cats, and then have to subsist on tuna fish for the rest of the week. Or she'd purchase wildly extravagant gifts like the diamond unicorn pin Becky had sent her sister for her birthday a few weeks ago, followed up with an urgent request for a loan. Fondly, Lauren fingered the pin on her lapel. She didn't even want to *think* how much the piece must have cost her sister. Or her latest boyfriend, she guessed wryly.

Men were always falling all over themselves to score points with the vivacious Becky. It wouldn't have surprised Lauren if her current love hadn't footed the bill for the expensive birthday gift. From

the way her sister had gushed about the guy, he
could afford it. According to her, Dave Jannisek was
as loaded as he was handsome. Becky had even
hinted that she might be serious about this one.

If so, it would be the first time she'd ever fallen
for one of her many admirers. Lauren suspected
their parents' bitter divorce and Lauren's own short,
disastrous marriage had given the volatile Becky a
permanent fear of commitment.

Finding her ex in bed with another woman had
certainly made Lauren herself wary of leading with
her heart instead of her head, but she didn't com-
pensate for that humbling experience by indulging
in a string of love-'em-and-leave-'em relationships
the way her sister did.

None of which explained where said sister was at
this particular moment. Or why her front door had
been standing open when Lauren arrived.

Raking her hand through the hair that was so like
her sister's in its thickness and dark red sheen, Lauren thought about that open door. The moment she'd
noticed it, alarms had started pinging up and down
her nervous system. Whatever or whoever had made
Becky so nervous was starting to make Lauren dis-
tinctly uncomfortable, as well.

She'd check the kitchen, she decided, tossing
aside the oversized tote that doubled as an over-
nighter for quick trips like this. Maybe she'd find
some clue to Becky's whereabouts there. If not,
she'd grab a shower, clean some of the clutter off
the bed, and zonk out until her sister showed up.

After the long flight from D.C. to Denver, followed by the hop down to Phoenix, even Lauren's jet lag had jet lag.

She was halfway out the door when she spotted what looked like the strap to Becky's favorite shoulder bag buried under a discarded blouse on the floor. Frowning, she pulled out the purse and checked its contents. Wadded tissues, loose half-sticks of cinnamon gum, a funky little makeup bag in the shape of a grinning Garfield and the embossed leather wallet Lauren had given her for Christmas a couple years ago. No house or car keys.

She hefted the wallet in her hand and looked inside. Fresh concern spilled through her. Why would her sister leave the house without her cash or credit cards?

Thinking of that open front door, Lauren slipped Becky's wallet into her own tote for safekeeping. She'd hang on to it until Beck showed up, or until Lauren figured out just what the heck was going on here.

Forehead creased with worry, she headed for the hall. She'd better call her assistant Josh. She'd have to cancel her early morning meeting with the stationery supplier who wanted to show her his new line of stock. If Becky showed up any time soon, maybe Lauren could still make her afternoon appointment with the director of Denver's museum of fine art. She really wanted the museum account.

Really *needed* that account.

An exclusive contract to produce the museum's

postcards and gift stationery could finally take her fledgling design firm out of the red. She'd launched the business after her divorce had left her jobless as well as husbandless. Drawing on her art training, she had decided to specialize in adapting the great masterpieces to local scenery. Her unique designs were just starting to take off, particularly the cards that blended the whimsical, mythical creatures she so loved into familiar settings.

Lauren had sunk everything she had into the enterprise. Everything she could scrape together, that is, after her ex had cleaned out their joint account. And Jack had had the nerve to look wounded when Lauren told him that she was reverting back to her maiden name. How had she ever imagined herself in love with the jerk?

Wondering if man trouble was what had precipitated Becky's odd call, Lauren headed down the narrow hall toward the kitchen.

The sound of glass shattering spun her around. Eyes wide, she stared at the front door. For a heart-stopping instant she caught a shadowy movement on the other side. Then, a black-gloved hand reached through the broken glass and groped for the dead bolt Lauren had locked behind her only minutes before.

Lauren didn't stop to think. Didn't even consider snatching up the phone to dial 911. Someone wanting in the front door was enough to send her flying down the hall and out the back. Her fingers frantic, she fumbled with the dead bolt on the kitchen door.

The knob wouldn't turn. It twisted halfway, then caught, as if the tumblers inside the lock were out of alignment or gummed up or something. She slammed a palm against the door and tried again.

"Come on! Come on!"

Still the dead bolt wouldn't turn the whole way. In a spurt of pure desperation, she tugged off her shoe and whacked at the bolt with the stacked heel, and then tried again.

The lock gave. Almost sobbing with relief, Lauren threw open the door and charged outside. Two steps later, she collided with a wall of solid muscle.

"What the hell…?"

The gruff voice split the darkness as Lauren rocked back, almost toppling over. Hard hands grabbed her arms, whether to save her from falling or to keep her from running, she had no idea. She flung her head up, gasped at the sight of the lean, shadowed face inches from hers.

"Are you okay?"

"I…—I…" Lauren struggled to reply around the lump in her throat.

Those hard fingers stayed locked around her upper arms, but the hold gentled, supporting her while she stammered incoherently.

"Who…? What…?"

"I'm your new neighbor. I was carrying some boxes out to the trash and heard the sound of glass shattering. Did you drop something? Cut yourself?"

Too flustered to correct his mistaken impression that she was Becky, Lauren did manage to gather

her scattered wits enough to register two swift impressions. One, his eyes were the bluest she'd ever seen. They reflected the light pouring from the kitchen like blue ice. Two, the hands wrapped around her arms were bare, uncovered by black gloves.

"Someone broke in the front door," she got out on a shaky breath. "He smashed the glass and reached inside to turn the dead bolt."

His head shot up. Eyes narrowed, he peered over her head at the house she'd just vacated.

"I left my back door open," he said tersely. "Go inside, shoot the lock behind you, and wait there until I get back."

Uncurling his hands, he started forward. Alarmed, Lauren snatched at the sleeve of his blue denim shirt.

"Wait! You can't go in there alone!"

He eased out of her grip. "It's okay. I know what I'm doing. Go on over to my place. I'll let you know when it's all clear."

His calm instruction almost convinced her that a little breaking and entering wasn't anything to get excited about. The wicked-looking automatic he slid out of a holster at the small of his back convinced her otherwise.

With swift efficiency, he ejected the magazine, checked the load and palmed it back in place. Swallowing, Lauren lifted her nervous gaze from the gun to his face.

"Shouldn't we just go to your place and call the police?"

"My phone's not hooked up yet."

He cocked the weapon, pulled back the slide and released it with a snap that ricocheted through the stillness. Then his white teeth flashed in a grin that was pure, rogue male.

"If it makes you feel any better, though, I *am* the police."

Chapter 2

Satisfaction sang in Marsh's veins as he went through the motions of searching Becky Smith's house. Judging by the target's stammering incoherence a moment ago, he'd achieved exactly the results he'd hoped for when he'd staged that bit of B and E. Good thing he'd thought to jimmy the dead bolt on the kitchen door. The stuck lock had given him the few moments he'd needed to rip off the black gloves, toss them into a handy bush and race around to the back of the house in time to intercept the woman who'd come flying out.

Sternly, Marsh repressed the twinge of guilt that tried to wiggle through his sharp satisfaction. Okay, he'd set her up. And yes, he fully intended to play on her stammering fear. If nothing else, the delectable Ms. Smith was guilty of associating with a gambler who was head over his heels in debt to the mob. She was up to her neck also in the dirty business that had led to Ellen's death. Marsh refused to let her frightened brown eyes deter him from finding his sister-in-law's killer. Now, if he could just shake the memory of Becky Smith's trembling body pressed against his, he could concentrate on finessing her into the next phase of his carefully constructed plan.

With a last glance at the mayhem that constituted her living room, he strode down the hall and out the back door. A frown sliced across his face when he spotted her crouched in the shadows of the hedge that separated her rented house from his. That wasn't part of his plan.

"Didn't I tell you to go inside my place and lock the door behind you?"

"I thought…" she began, straightening up. "That is, I was worried you might need help."

"Help?" He threw a disbelieving glance at the garbage can lid she gripped in one hand. "What the hell did you think you could accomplish with that?"

"Well, I was thinking along the lines of bonking the intruder over the head if he came running out. But I probably wouldn't have had the nerve to do much more than make a racket and scare him off," she admitted, dropping the lid back on the can.

The fact that she'd been prepared to take a stand at all surprised Marsh. From everything he'd learned about Becky Smith, she'd struck him as more likely to turn tail and run at the first sign of trouble, the way she did after the police interviewed her a few days ago.

"Is he…?" She darted a look at her back door. "Is he gone?"

"He's gone." Marsh slid his Glock back into its holster at the small of his back. "He must have wanted in pretty bad, though, to bust the glass like that instead of taking the time to use a cutter or lock pick. Any idea what he was after, Miss Smith?"

She shook her head, her nervous gaze still on her sister's house.

She didn't blink at his use of her name, or ask how he knew it. Marsh had an explanation all ready. He'd even been prepared to lecture her on the idiocy of stenciling her last name as well as the house number on the mailbox out front. Since neither the explanation nor the lecture appeared necessary, he dug the hook in a little deeper.

"I thought I heard a car pull up in front a few moments ago. Was that you?"

Distracted, she shoved a hand through her hair. "Yes. I took a cab. From the airport."

His pulse jumped. The cop in him almost asked her where she'd flown in from. The patient, determined hunter knew better than to press too hard or too fast. Instead, he used the truth to spring his trap of lies.

"Whoever tried to break in must have seen you drive up. Sounds as if he was waiting for you."

Her head jerked up. "Waiting? For me?"

Marsh steeled himself against the shock that leaped into her eyes. ''I'd say it was a distinct possibility.''

Every bit of the color she'd recovered drained from her face.

Ruthlessly, Marsh clamped down on his feeling of guilt. If she insisted on making it with guys who played games with the mob, she'd better be prepared to face a few unpleasantries in life. Curling a hand around her upper arm, he steered her toward her back door.

''I could be wrong. Maybe it was just a kid wanting something to pawn. You'd better take a look and see if anything's missing.''

Lauren almost told him that she'd already looked, and that she had no idea what, if anything, might be missing. The words stuck in her throat, unable to get past the thick lump of fear and dismay he'd lodged there.

Had someone been waiting for Becky? Was there something more sinister behind her sister's disjointed message than mere man trouble? Her thoughts tumbled chaotically.

Lauren reentered the house she'd charged out of just moments ago. Once inside, she whirled to face Becky's neighbor, intending to pour out the details of her sister's phone call.

''I...''

His narrow, fiercely intent expression killed the impulse on the spot. He looked like a hawk, she thought, in the fleeting instant before he blanked his expression. Or one of those blue-eyed timber wolves who ranged the Rockies. Sharp. Predatory. Dangerous.

"You what?"

"I, uh…"

She tried to shake the ridiculous imagery. He was a cop, for Pete's sake! A police officer!

Or so he'd said.

Thoroughly disconcerted by her sudden, leaping doubts, Lauren tried to think of a tactful way to ask the man who'd just rushed to her rescue for some form of identification.

She must have looked as confused as she felt at that moment. His narrowed gaze swept over her face.

"Are you all right, Miss Smith?"

Belatedly, she recalled that he still thought she was Becky. With the realization came an instinctive decision to let him continue to think so until she sorted out just what she'd walked into. The mile-wide protective streak the two sisters had always felt for each had now kicked in, big time.

Older than Lauren by a scant ten months, a youthful Becky had tried to shield her sister from their parents' bitter break up with her determined cheerfulness and refusal to cry. On more nights than Lauren wanted to remember, the two girls had huddled together in bed, trying to close their ears to the shouting, the scathing recriminations, the slamming doors. The long summer they'd spent with their mother's friend, Jane, while their parents waged a bitter war for custody, had cemented the girls' affection for each other into an indestructible force.

As they'd grown older, their roles had reversed. Solemn, focused Lauren had worked her way though high school and college, while Becky dropped out after her freshman year and flitted from city to city, man to man. Lauren was always there when her sister needed a loan or a place to camp out.

Just as Becky had been there for Lauren after she'd walked in on her husband and their accountant, and then turned around and walked out of her marriage.

Blood ran thicker than a dented heart, and the bond between the sisters ran thicker than blood.

"Yes, I'm all right," she replied to this watching, watchful neighbor. "Just...nervous, I guess."

He nodded, the movement a mere dip of his head.

The overhead light caught the glints in his dark hair. He wore it cut short, Lauren noted, neat and trim as a police officer might.

He had the body of a cop, too, or at least the body of one of those heartthrob TV cops. Broad shoulders strained the seams of his blue denim shirt. Sleeves rolled halfway up displayed arms corded with muscle. His jeans rode low on a washboard-flat belly.

As Lauren had learned from her brief, disastrous foray into marriage, however, great pecs and a flat stomach didn't count for squat when it came to character. Her ex, Jack, had worked out regularly—not that his carefully cultivated physique could compare to this rugged, square-jawed stranger's.

"Are you up to doing a walk-through?" he asked, those arctic blue eyes filled with seeming concern.

Needing the time to sort through her chaotic thoughts, Lauren nodded and turned to lead the way down the hall.

With her protective instincts now on full alert, she couldn't miss the sardonic twist to his mouth when she flipped on the lights to the living room. Bristling inwardly on Becky's behalf, she followed his gaze as it swept the room.

The mess epitomized her sister's lack of roots and constant job-hopping as much as her casual approach to housekeeping. The furniture had obviously come with the rented house. A blend of desert chic and cheap sturdiness, it consisted of a sofa and two chairs cushioned in shades of mauve and turquoise, one end table and a tacky, cactus-shaped lamp. The collection of orange-striped Garfield cats that crowded the shelf above an adobe fireplace gave the room Becky's distinctive stamp.

More than anything else, the grinning cats spoke to the differences between the sisters. Lauren specialized in fine works of art and mythical creatures like unicorns and dragons and griffins. Becky collected Garfields. And frothy underwear...like the lavender silk teddy trimmed in black lace draped over the arm of the chair.

It was just the type of thing Becky loved to wear, skimpy up top and even skimpier below. Becky had tried to talk her more conservative younger sister into the same thong-style undergarments a number of times, but Lauren had never mastered the art of sitting down in the darned things without squirming.

She might have guessed that the man beside her wouldn't miss the provocative teddy. His glance zinged from the lavender silk to Lauren.

"At least we know the intruder wasn't some pervert after your underwear," he said, with just the hint of a drawl. "He wouldn't have left that little number behind. Assuming he could find it in this mess."

The half joke, half barb brought her chin up. She might complain about the untidiness every time she came to visit, but only a sister could claim that prerogative.

Her smile turned saccharine sweet. Slanting her best Becky glance from under her lashes, she purred out a sharp little jab of her own.

"Do you have a problem with the decorating scheme, big guy? Or maybe you're wondering how that teddy got left in the living room?"

That grabbed his attention. Startled, he stared down at her. For a moment Lauren had the satisfaction of knowing she'd scored a point. Exactly what that point was, or why she'd suddenly felt the need to score one, she had no idea.

"No problem," he replied, flashing another heart-stopping grin, even more potent than the one he'd laid on her in the backyard. "With either the decor or where you shed your clothes."

Lauren was still trying to recover from that dazzling combination of white teeth, tanned skin and

uncensored male when he hooked a thumb toward
the bedroom.

"Why don't we finish going through the house?"

Marsh's grin faded the moment she turned away.
His jaw tightened as he gave himself a swift, silent
mental kick in the butt. Her sugar-coated smile and
playful little jibe had caught him completely off
guard. They'd also started him thinking about things
he shouldn't be thinking about...such as just when
and how Becky Smith had shimmied out of that
teddy.

He'd damn well better control his reactions
around this bit of fluff. He couldn't let her throw
him with those kittenish glances or melting brown
eyes. There was too much riding on the next few
hours for Marsh to blow everything now.

What he couldn't seem to control, however, was
his imagination, which threatened to take off with
each seductive sway of Becky Smith's hips. She
moved like the strawberry roan filly that had grown
into her legs the summer Marsh turned fifteen. Her
stride was all smooth, swaying magic. And her backside...

He reined in that thought, fast. It stood to reason
that she'd look as good from behind as she did from
the front. She'd seduced Jannisek with one swish of
her short, ruffled cocktail skirt, or so her various co-
workers at the Desert Nights Lounge maintained.
According to them, the hotel owner had fallen fast
and he'd fallen hard.

Fast enough to make his employees smirk when they described it.

Hard enough to shell out two thousand dollars for the diamond pin his girlfriend sported on her lapel.

She was wearing Jannisek's brand, Marsh reminded himself grimly. The man had staked a claim to her. And he'd come looking for her when she didn't return to wherever he waited for her.

Marsh was counting on it. *He* sure as hell would come after her. If Marsh had claimed this woman and put his own mark on her, she couldn't run fast enough or far enough to escape him.

Unless he let her go.

He tensed, anticipating the little jab of pain that always came with the reminder of how he'd let Jenna go. His shoulders went stiff, the way they did whenever he thought of his former fiancée. As if it had a will of its own, his mind reached back to those weeks he'd hovered between life and death. To the agony that came with each breath pulled into his bullet-riddled lung. To the woman who'd fallen apart every time she came to visit him in intensive care.

If he let himself, Marsh knew he could summon in precise detail Jenna's tear-streaked face. Still hear her sobs as she told him she couldn't marry a cop, couldn't worry whether she'd see her husband again every time he left for work.

Deliberately, Marsh slammed the door on the memories. Four years had passed since Jenna had walked out of the hospital, three and a half since

Marsh had fully recovered. She'd married a nice, safe junior-high science teacher. Life went on....

Except for Ellen.

The grim reminder brought Marsh's thoughts crashing back to the disaster zone Becky Smith called a bedroom.

This time, he didn't react with so much as a blink to the chaos. He'd seen the bedroom before, for one thing. For another, he was more interested in Becky than her lack of anything resembling order in her home. Face impassive, he waited while she made a quick survey of the room's contents.

"I don't think anything's missing."

Moving with seeming nonchalance, Marsh lifted a gold bracelet from the dressing table. Another Garfield dangled from the center link, this one made of gold and crystal.

"A thief wouldn't have passed up this piece. It looks expensive."

"It was a gift." Her eyes clouded. "From my sister."

"You shouldn't leave expensive jewelry like this lying around. Take that pin you're wearing. If those are real diamonds, it should go into a safe place at night."

Her hand lifted to the sparkling piece. He moved closer, as if to examine the design.

"What is it, a unicorn?"

"Yes."

"Do you believe in the legend, Ms. Smith?"

"About those who drink out of its horn being protected from poison or epilepsy?"

"I didn't know that one."

She tipped her head to the side, studying him with the same intent scrutiny he gave her. "Which legend are you talking about, then?"

Her hair danced on her shoulder like dark flame. Marsh pulled his gaze from the shimmering curtain. "I seem to remember reading somewhere that only a virgin could capture and tame a unicorn."

Actually, he remembered exactly where he'd read that bit of nonsense—on the sales brochure the jewelry-store clerk had provided the police.

Her head dipped in acknowledgment. "True. That was supposed to symbolize the triumph of spiritual love over the ferocity of the beast. Too bad it's only a myth," she added, with a twist to her mouth that didn't quite make it to a smile.

Obviously Ms. Smith didn't believe in the power or permanency of love. That certainly fit her profile. In the past eighteen months, she'd taken up with a tattooed motorcycle jock and a drummer in a country western band before latching on to Jannisek—an association that might just get her killed.

Carefully, Marsh repositioned the bracelet on the nightstand. "If the man who broke through the glass wasn't after jewelry..."

"Or some pervert after underwear," she interjected coolly.

"...then I'd say we were right the first time. It was you he was waiting for—you he wanted."

She caught her lower lip between her teeth. Marsh refused to follow the movement of that raspberry-tinted mouth. Refused to let her nervousness sway him.

"Why did he wait outside?" she questioned, thinking back. "The front door was open when I got here. He could have walked inside."

"Maybe he did. Maybe he searched the place, saw you weren't here, and was on his way out again when the cab pulled up."

And maybe he wanted to scare you enough to make sure you reacted the way you did. Reminding himself yet again that shaking up Becky Smith constituted an essential part of his plan, Marsh ignored the nervous way she had crossed her arms and rubbed her hands up and down her sleeves.

"Why would someone come after you, Ms. Smith? Or should I call you Becky?" He aimed a smile at her. "We are neighbors, after all."

"Um…"

He took that vague response as consent. "Any ideas, Becky?"

"About what?"

"Who might come after you? And why?"

He kept his tone even and nonthreatening, but every nerve in Marsh's body quivered in anticipation of her reply. She took her time about it, dropping her lids, glancing away, looking everywhere but at him. Thinking, obviously, how she would answer.

"I don't know," she said at last.

Disappointment whipped through him. A part of him had hoped she'd cooperate voluntarily, and that he wouldn't have to implement Phase Three.

He didn't see any other option now. He angled his head, his gaze thoughtful as it rested on her face.

"You can tell me. In my line of work, I've seen about every kind of trouble people can get into."

She took her lower lip between her teeth again. Marsh figured she would chew off a couple of layers of skin before he got through with her. Her chocolate and caramel eyes searched his face.

"I don't know your name."

The abrupt change in direction threw him off stride for a moment. "What?"

"I don't know who you are," she said again.

"Henderson. Marsh Henderson."

"Or what you are," she added slowly.

"I told you. I'm a cop."

"Do you have some identification?"

He blinked, and then gave a snort of laughter. "Isn't it a little late to be asking to see my badge?"

Her chin came up. "You know what they say, Mr. Henderson..."

"Marsh."

"You know what they say, Marsh. Better late than too late."

His mouth kicked up in a half grin. "That's what they say, all right."

Digging into his back pocket, he pulled out a black leather case. A single flip displayed his photo

ID and gold badge with its blue enamel shield, sur-
mounted by an open-winged gold eagle.

"U.S." She read the large initials in the center of
the shield easily enough, but squinted at the smaller
lettering around it. "U.S. what?"

"U.S. Drug Enforcement Agency. I'm a special
agent with the DEA."

"A special agent?" she echoed, paling.

Obviously, his profession made her nervous. It
made a lot of people nervous. As it should, Marsh
thought sardonically. Flipping the leather case shut,
he slid it into his back pocket.

"I get the feeling you're wondering just why I
happened to move into the house next door."

"Maybe I am."

"Smart lady."

"Well?"

"We've been using the place to conduct a surveillance." He kept his eyes locked with hers.
"We've been watching your house for the past three
days, Becky, waiting for you to come home."

The "we" was stretching things, but the target
didn't need to know that.

"Why?" she whispered.

"To take you into protective custody."

Chapter 3

"**P**rotective custody!"

Stunned, Lauren gaped at the man staring down at her.

"Why?" she asked, for what seemed like the hundredth time in the past few minutes.

"Because you're our only link to David Jannisek."

Becky's latest love. The man she just might be serious about. With a shake of her head, Lauren tried to grasp what the heck this was all about.

"Why do you want to find Jannisek?"

His face seemed to get tighter around the edges. "You know why."

"No, I don't."

Henderson's eyes went ice cold. Lauren could feel the chill from where she stood.

"Your boyfriend has had a run of bad luck at the track recently. Our sources tell us he owes his bookie more than five hundred."

"Five hundred dollars?"

"Try five hundred grand."

"Good God!"

Was that why Becky needed time to think things through? She'd fallen for a loser—just as her sister had? If so, Lauren ached for her. She could speak firsthand to that painful experience.

"He liquidated every asset he owned," Henderson continued, wrenching her attention back to him. "Didn't you wonder what happened to his Jag?"

Or didn't you care? his expression seemed to imply. His gaze flicked to Lauren's lapel once again, telegraphing an unmistakably cynical message.

"Your boyfriend blew the last of his credit on that little bauble. The store clerk said Jannisek told him to spread the cost of it over three separate charge cards, all of which maxed out."

Lauren felt herself squirming on Becky's behalf. Her sister didn't have a greedy bone in her body, but there was no denying she was careless about finances—her own and everyone else's. She never hesitated to hit Lauren up for a loan. And she'd apparently walked out of her house without her checkbook and credit cards! She probably didn't have a clue that her latest love interest was up to his neck in financial hot water.

"Is that why you're after him?" Lauren asked,

still trying to comprehend this bizarre situation. "Because of what he owes?"

"I don't care what he owes. It's who he owes it to that I'm interested in."

From the set of Henderson's mouth, Lauren had the feeling that matters were about to go from bad to worse for David Jannisek—and, by extension, for her sister. Digging her fists into her jacket pockets, she braced herself.

"All right. Lay it on me. Who does he owe it to?"

"The man we suspect of controlling organized crime in the Southwest."

"Organized crime?" Her jaw dropped. "You mean, like, the mafia?"

"The modern-day version of it."

She was still reeling from that when he closed the distance between them, his boot heels thudding softly on the wooden floor.

Lauren took an instinctive step back. From across the room, Marsh Henderson projected a sizzling masculinity. Up close and personal, he was just a little bit intimidating.

Okay, more than a little. Except…

He hadn't *felt* intimidating when she'd plowed into him in the backyard. For a few moments there, he'd felt strong and solid and safe.

"That's the man I want," he told her, his deep voice resonating with an intensity that raised goose bumps on her arms. "The mob boss. And you're going to help me nail him, Becky."

"How?"

"By letting me tuck you away in a nice, safe place. If Jannisek's half as much in love with you as everyone says he is, he'll come looking for you."

"In other words," she said slowly, incredulously, "you want to set a trap?"

"Yes."

"With...with me as bait?"

"Yes."

The blunt admission ignited a little curl of anger deep in Lauren's chest. It hadn't taken this tough-edged cop long to show his stripes. He didn't care about her sister. Didn't care about David Jannisek. All he wanted was to bring down this shadowy mobster. So much for solid and safe!

"And when Jannisek comes looking for the woman he supposedly loves," she ground out, "he'll find you instead."

"That's the plan."

"At which point, you'll convince him to identify the man you say he owes so much money to." Her nails dug into her palms. "What if he doesn't want to cooperate?"

"As I see it, he doesn't have a whole lot of choice in the matter. He'll either cooperate, or spend the rest of his life dodging bullets."

Shocked, Lauren took a step back. Henderson followed, relentless.

"That shook you up, didn't it? To have the police show up at your door and inform you that Jannisek missed taking a clip full of bullets by a few turns of a car wheel?''

"I... I didn't...''

He crowded in closer. "He'd just dropped you off, hadn't he? A minute or two earlier, and you could have been sitting beside him when the bullets started flying. No wonder you skipped town for a few days.''

Oh, God! This was worse, so much worse, than Lauren had imagined. Poor Becky. She must be scared to death. It was time to set the record straight.

"Look, Henderson...''

"Marsh,'' he corrected with a tight smile. "If we're going to spend the foreseeable future in close proximity, we might as well get comfortable with each other.''

"We won't be spending the future in any kind of proximity. You've made a mistake. I'm not Becky Smith.''

He went still. Completely still. The air around them took on a charged tension. The seconds ticked by while Lauren's nerves stretched wire thin.

"The hell you're not,'' he growled at last.

"I'm her sister. Lauren Smith.''

Those incredible blue eyes narrowed to slits, dropped lower, settled on the diamond unicorn. When they lifted again, Lauren read scorn and flat denial in their depths.

"Nice try, Becky, but it won't work. You're coming with me.''

"Oh, for...!'' Turning, she snatched her tote off

the bed. "I'm not going anywhere with you. I have…"

Her breath left with a squeak when Henderson ripped the bag out of her hands. She stumbled back, realizing belatedly that the cop thought she might have been reaching for a weapon.

"My driver's license," she gasped. "It's in there. It will prove I'm not…. Oh!"

Groaning, she recognized the hand-tooled leather clutch he dug out.

"That's not mine!"

He shot her a sardonic look, flipped open the wallet and compared the grainy, three-year-old picture on Becky's Arizona license to Lauren's stricken face.

"Not your best shot," he drawled.

"That's—not—me," she ground out. "That's my sister. If you dig a little deeper, you'll find a day planner with *my* license and credit cards inside."

When he pulled out the zippered notebook, a frown sliced across his face. It deepened to a scowl as his glance went from the photo to her face and back again.

Lauren cringed inwardly. She took horrible pictures. She'd shied away from family photos, even as a child, maybe because her parents' marriage had started to fall apart so early and group pictures had always seemed forced. Whatever the reason, she always froze in front of a camera. The photo on her license was even worse than Becky's.

"Sit down."

She blinked at the abrupt command. "I don't..."

"Sit down!"

Lauren decided that discretion was the better part of valor at this point and sat.

"Don't move until I get back," he snarled, tossing the tote down beside her. "I'm going to the other room to make a few calls."

Her heart pumping, she watched him stride out of the bedroom. A moment later, she caught a muffled snatch of conversation.

Who could he call to verify her identity? she wondered wildly. The phone at her office would ring unanswered. There was no one at her condo. She leaned forward, straining to hear the deep rumble of Henderson's voice.

"...run an ID for me. Right now, Pepper. I'll hang on."

Wrapping her arms around her waist, Lauren rocked back and forth on the edge of the bed while her thoughts tumbled chaotically. How in the world had Becky gotten tangled up with someone who had ties to the mob? Would they really come after her, thinking she'd lead them to this Jannisek character?

Oh, God, would they hurt her? Maybe kill her?

She had to convince Henderson he had the wrong sister, had to get him looking for the right one. When he got off the phone, Lauren would get on. She'd call their parents, now divorced and living on separate coasts. Contact their aunt Jane. Check with her assistant, Josh. Maybe Becky had gotten in touch with one of them. Maybe she'd left a message....

She jerked upright. Her gaze shot to the tote.

"Idiot!"

Her heart pounding, Lauren yanked open the side zipper on her tote. The mobile phone that always traveled with her nestled in its snug compartment. She had the lid up and the first few digits of her home number punched in before she noticed the message on the digital display.

She had voice mail.

Chewing on her lip, she debated for all of two seconds before dialing the code to retrieve her message. When she heard Becky's voice asking her to call an unfamiliar number as soon as possible, she almost wept with relief. Her fingers shook as she punched in the digits.

"Joe's Joint," a nasal-sounding individual answered.

"Joe's *what?*"

"Who's this?"

She threw a look at the bedroom door and lowered her voice. Henderson's last threat still crawled along her spine. "Who are you?"

"Whadda you playin' games or something, lady?"

"No! No, I..." She stopped, regrouped her thoughts. "Is there a woman named Becky, or Rebecca, Smith there? She's twenty-six, has shoulder-length red hair."

"Becky? Yeah, she's here. You wanna talk to her?"

"Yes!"

Her heart thumping, Lauren kept the cellphone jammed to one ear and the other tuned to the murmur of Henderson's voice.

"Hey, Laur," her sister answered a moment later.

"Where are you!"

"At a truck stop outside Gallup."

"Gallup, as in New Mexico?"

"You got it."

"What in the world are you doing there?"

"Well, I was on my way to your place, but I remembered you were in D.C., so I decided to detour by way of Albuquerque to visit Aunt Jane until you got back. Only I'm, uh, in sort of a bind."

"No kidding!"

"I know, I know." She chuckled into the phone. "I'm always in some kind of a bind."

How could she laugh? Lauren wondered in astonishment. Didn't she know a hard-eyed cop was after her? Maybe the mob?

Apparently not. As it turned out, Becky's most pressing concern at that moment was that she'd driven off with only the cash in her pocket—which had now run out.

"Be a sweetie and wire me a hundred, would you? I'll pay you back when I get to Denver."

"I'm not in Denver. I'm in Phoenix, at your place."

"You're kidding!"

"I wish I was. Becky, this David Jannisek. Do you know he's in trouble?"

The chipper note in her sister's voice dimmed. "Yes. That's why I had to get away for a while. I thought...I thought I knew him. I was sure I could trust him."

From her own bitter experience, Lauren could have pointed out that knowing a man and trusting him were two entirely different matters.

Take this Marsh Henderson, for example. She might have trusted him. She'd *wanted* to trust him. His blunt admission that he intended to use her sister as bait had nipped that misplaced impulse in the bud. Now that she knew Becky was safe, Lauren's protective instincts were fast revving up to full power.

"Beck, listen to me. Forget about going to my apartment. That's the first place they'll look for you."

"Who?"

"Jannisek's gangster friends. The police. They're both after him. And you."

"Me!" she squeaked. "Why me?"

"They think he might come out of hiding for you."

"Oh, God!"

"Listen, I don't have time to explain any more right now. I'll call Josh and have him wire you some money. Go on to Aunt Jane's and stay there."

Their mother's best friend. The woman the Smith sisters had stayed with that awful summer of their parents' divorce. Jane wasn't actually a blood relation. No one would connect her with Becky. Her sister was safe there until Lauren got this mess with the police sorted out.

She didn't even stop to consider that it wasn't her mess to sort out. She'd jumped into every crisis Becky had precipitated over the years without a second thought. She wasn't about to let anyone use her sister as bait.

"Stay there, okay?"

"But..."

The thud of footsteps sent Lauren's heartbeat into a spike. "I'll call you!" she whispered urgently and snapped the phone shut. It slid into the tote just seconds before Henderson loomed in the doorway.

"Well?" she asked with what she hoped was credible nonchalance.

"I've verified that a Lauren Smith lives at 2205 Crescent Drive," he growled. "That doesn't necessarily prove you're Lauren Smith."

She pushed off the bed, her relief at making contact with her sister shoved to the background by this flint-edged cop's unwillingness to accept the facts in front of his face.

"If I'm Becky, what am I doing with Lauren's wallet?"

"If you're Lauren," he fired back, "what are you doing with Becky's?"

"She left it here. I just picked it up for safekeeping."

"Right."

"I don't believe this."

Totally frustrated, Lauren speared a hand through her hair. Her closest brush with the law was a parking ticket three years ago. She'd paid the fine promptly and always maintained a healthy respect for police officers. But Henderson's subtly veiled threats and flat refusal to accept her assertion that she wasn't her sister punched all the wrong buttons. She had rights, didn't she? So did Becky. Lauren was still formulating those rights in her mind when Henderson blew them away.

"I'm going with the hard evidence here," he said on a tight note. "You walked into Becky's house like it was your own. You're wearing the pin Becky's boyfriend shelled out two thousand dollars for. You're carrying Becky's ID. You're Becky Smith, lady, unless or until someone says otherwise."

"All right," she fumed. "What if I am Becky? That still doesn't mean I have to go anywhere with you."

"Guess again."

"I beg your pardon?"

"I'd prefer your cooperation," he said, his voice flat and uncompromising, "but we can do this the hard way if necessary."

"What are you going to do?" she scoffed. "Slap on some handcuffs and haul me in?"

"If I have to."

Lauren brought her chin up. "On what charges?

Since when is getting involved with the wrong man against the law?''

A mistake, maybe. A *big* mistake if you ended up married to the cretin. But against the law? She didn't think so.

"Try obstruction of justice," he shot back. "Hindering a law enforcement officer in the performance of his duty. Being a material witness in an ongoing criminal investigation."

That got her attention. So did the acerbic observation he tacked on.

"You know, you ought to be more careful about who you get 'involved' with. You seem to have a propensity for the wrong men."

Her chin came up another notch. "Been checking into my sister's colorful past, have you?"

"I've been checking into *Becky Smith's* past," he countered. "She's left a string of broken hearts all across the Southwest."

As he reeled off a list of her sister's recent affairs, Lauren's temper came to a slow boil. She knew how deeply their parents' acrimonious break up had scarred her sibling, and how gun-shy Becky'd grown about commitment. With the sting of her own divorce fading but not forgotten, Lauren wasn't exactly anxious to jump off the deep end with another male any time soon, either. Her jaw tightened as Henderson issued another of his brusque orders.

"Pack enough to get you through the next few days."

"Let's try this again. You've got the wrong woman."

"Is that so? Then where's the right one?"

"She's...she's safe."

He crossed the room in three swift strides. Lauren felt her heart thud against her ribs as a suddenly, startlingly dangerous man towered over her.

"Where is she? With Jannisek?"

"No!"

"How do you know?"

Lauren decided not to reveal the fact that she had a phone tucked in her purse. "I just do."

"So you've been stringing me along here, is that it?"

He looked so fierce, she almost caved and told him she'd sent Becky to Aunt Jane's. But Lauren wasn't going to offer her sister up as anyone's sacrificial goat. Her mouth clamped shut.

Another silence stretched between them. Henderson finally broke it, his eyes like chips of ice.

"Pack what you'll need for a few days," he ordered again.

"But...!"

"If you're Becky Smith, you're not safe here. If you're *not* Becky Smith, you're still not safe here. We have to assume the guys looking for your boyfriend are looking for her, too. They might make the same mistake in identities you say I did."

Lauren was beginning to appreciate how Alice in Wonderland must have felt after tumbling down the rabbit hole. She wasn't sure of anything anymore—

except that the idea of spending the next few days in the protective custody of Special Agent Henderson sent a nervous ripple across her skin.

"I'll get my car," he informed her tersely. "Meet me out back in five minutes."

He turned away, took two strides, swung back again.

"If you're thinking about trying to run out the front door, don't. I'd be on you like mud on a mustang before you got a half a block."

Lauren's back teeth ground together. "I'm going to say this one more time. You're making a mistake."

"Maybe. Maybe not."

Still fuming, she listened to his footsteps retreat down the hall. Only after her anger cooled did the awful reality of the situation sink in. The idea that some thugs might be searching for her sister left a sick feeling in Lauren's stomach.

Poor Becky! She'd have to stay in hiding indefinitely. Unless...

Unless someone drew the dogs off her scent. Someone like her sister.

Lauren gulped. Marsh Henderson had mistaken her for Becky. Others often did, too. Maybe... maybe she *could* stand in for Becky. Take Henderson up on his offer of protection while his associates hunted down this mobster who was supposedly after her boyfriend.

Biting on a fingernail, she tried desperately to think of other options. There weren't any that she could see. With a sigh of resignation, she dug in her purse for her cellphone again. Every beat of her heart sounded like thunder in her ears as she punched in her assistant's home number. He answered on the third ring.

"Josh, this is Lauren."

"Are you home?"

"No. I'm in Phoenix."

"I take it Becky's in a jam again."

"Sort of. I need you to wire her two hundred dollars. Send it in care of Joe's Joint, Gallup, New Mexico."

"What's she doing in Gallup? No, let me guess. She's taken up with a trucker this time."

Lauren let the caustic remark pass without comment. Josh still hadn't recovered from the time Becky had seduced him into a brief affair during one of her intermittent stays with Lauren. Beck had breezed off again a week later with a smile and a wave. Josh hadn't quite reached the smiling stage yet.

"Just wire the money, okay?"

"Okay, okay. Anything else?"

Lauren clenched the phone. "Yes. Cancel my appointments for the next few days."

"What?" His squawk jumped across the airwaves. "You've got that meeting with the museum director tomorrow afternoon! You know how important that is. And we promised some prototype note cards to the Breckinridge Group by Friday, remember?"

"I know."

She thought furiously. She'd spent hours on various sketches that incorporated world-famous art with the stag antlers that symbolized the equally world-famous Breckinridge Resort. Josh could start the process that would transform her sketches into polished products.

"I've worked up a dozen or so preliminary designs for the Breckinridge account. Scan them into the computer tomorrow and start working the color screens, will you? I'll get back as soon as I can."

"As soon as you can?" Disgust rippled through Josh's voice. "What the heck kind of mess has your twit of a sister left for you to clean up this time?"

"I can't explain now. I've got to go."

He was still grumbling when Lauren flipped the phone shut and dropped it back in her tote.

Now what?

She toyed briefly with the idea of calling a lawyer. Unfortunately, she didn't know an attorney other than the one who'd handled her divorce three years ago.

She was on her own with Henderson, who still didn't know whether she was Becky or not. The next few days could prove prickly at best, downright uncomfortable at worst.

Reluctantly, she crossed the room and pulled some tops, an Arizona Suns T-shirt and another pair of jeans from a jumble of clean laundry. They wouldn't fit in her tote, so she stuffed them in a canvas bag sporting the logo of the Hard Bodies

Gym and Sports Facility she found in Becky's
closet. A foray into her sister's underwear drawer
resulted in a handful of thong panties and matching
demi-bras. Grimacing, Lauren dumped them in with
the jeans and tops. Luckily, she'd packed a toothbrush and a few toiletries in her tote before she'd
left Denver. She was just adding a pair of sneakers
to the gym bag when Henderson's voice rang out.

"Ready?"

As ready as she'd ever be, she thought glumly.
Hefting the bags, she left the bedroom. At the sight
of Marsh Henderson striding toward her, she
stopped short.

He'd pulled on a suede vest lined with curly
sheep's wool. A black Stetson shadowed his eyes
and cheeks, already darkened with a day's growth
of beard. He looked big and tough—and a whole lot
more like an outlaw than a sheriff.

"I've got someone coming to repair the front
door," he informed her. "We'll go out the back."

When he reached for the gym bag and took it out
of Lauren's hands, she had the uncomfortable feeling she'd just relinquished more than a change of
clothes. Nerves prickling, she paced ahead of him
into the yard. A million stars spangled the sky, but
the black velvet night had a cool desert bite to it
that made her shiver under her light linen jacket.

A mud-splashed sports utility vehicle rumbled
like a nervous beast in the driveway separating the
two houses. It was one of those big jobs, and obviously more than just a nineties yuppie status sym-

bol. This monster came equipped with a wrap-around bush guard, fog lamps and a high-powered spotlight bolted to the driver's side.

Henderson opened the passenger door and tossed the gym bag over the high-backed front seat. Impatience radiated from him in almost palpable waves as he waited for her to climb in.

She approached the vehicle with a noticeable lack of enthusiasm. "Where are we going?"

"Given your boyfriend's connections..."

"He's *not* my boyfriend. He's Becky's. Or he was, until he got her into this mess."

"Given Jannisek's connections," Henderson amended without a blink, "I decided it was best to get you out of the area."

"How far out of the area?"

"I've arranged a safe house on a ranch up around Flagstaff."

As best Lauren remembered, the northern Arizona city was a hundred plus miles north of Phoenix and its surrounding suburbs. That meant two or more hours closed in this vehicle with Marsh Henderson, and who knew how many days with him on some ranch.

Praying she was doing the right thing, she pulled herself up onto the high step and dropped into the leather seat.

The passenger door closed with a thud.

Chapter 4

Marsh kept a death grip on the leather-wrapped steering wheel as he tooled the Blazer through Scottsdale's darkened streets. His mind whirled at even faster revolutions than the steel-belted tires.

Who the hell was sitting next to him? Becky Smith or her sister, Lauren? How long would it take his partner to run down her true identity? Twenty-four hours? Less? Did it matter?

Marsh's jaw clenched at the cold-blooded proposition that he could use either sister in the next phase of his plan, but he forced himself to consider it.

If this was Lauren—and if she could be believed—she knew where her sister was. She'd sworn Becky wasn't with Jannisek. Marsh had fired that

question too fast and her denial had come out too
spontaneously to be faked. So there was a chance,
a slim chance, that Jannisek had no idea what was
going down.

If, on the other hand, this woman was lying, and
she really was Becky, Marsh could proceed exactly
as planned.

So it boiled down to two choices. He could use
this woman, whoever she was, in a desperate attempt
to lure Jannisek out of hiding. Or he could accept
the Phoenix PD's decision to put the hunt for Ellen's
killers on the back burner.

Marsh didn't even consider the second option.
With a flick of a directional signal, he cut off Scottsdale Road onto Camelback. The Blazer whipped
past posh condos constructed to look like abode
dwellings and the sprawling resorts that made Phoenix the winter escape for millionaires and mobsters.

It was an area Marsh now knew well. Ellen's best
friend owned a condo in the shadow of the city's
legendary Camelback Mountain. Ellen had been on
her way for a visit and a day of shopping with her
friend when she'd been gunned down only a few
blocks away.

"Where are we going?"

The question dragged Marsh's thoughts from his
sister-in-law's bullet-riddled car and Jake's frozen
face as he watched Ellen's casket being lowered into
the Arizona earth. He speared a glance at the woman
beside him.

"I told you, to a ranch up by Flagstaff."

She took her lower lip between her teeth, and then twisted to catch a street sign. The movement brought her rear up hard against his thigh. With some effort, Marsh blanked his mind to the sudden, scorching pressure.

"We're heading west, not north."

Suspicion rang sharp in her voice. Obviously, she didn't trust him. Wise woman.

"We have to make a short stop before we head north."

"Where?"

"At the Valley of the Sun Inn."

"That's where my sister works! They'll verify that you've got the wrong woman."

"That's where Becky Smith works," he agreed. "Whether or not I have the wrong woman remains to be seen."

She folded her arms and stared straight ahead, her mouth set. She had, Marsh conceded with a swift, sideways glance, one helluva mouth. The kind a man could feast on. For hours. The body that went with it wasn't bad, either.

His fists tightened on the wheel. Who was he kidding? She'd rocked him onto his heels when she'd flung herself into his arms there at the house, and the impact had nothing to do with the hundred and twenty-three pounds her license said she carried on that perfectly proportioned frame.

Even now, with his mind spinning like a rat on a wheel, his senses insisted on working their own agenda. Much as Marsh wanted to deny it, Becky/

Lauren Smith knocked the breath back in his chest every time he pulled in her scent, an elusive combination of shampoo, seductive perfume and nervous woman. Those long legs that were stretched out beside his didn't exactly help his concentration, either. His fingers itched to hit the window button and drag some sharp night air into the Blazer to diffuse her impact on his senses. He needed all his wits to pull off the next, delicate step in his swiftly revised plan.

His passenger didn't know it yet, but he didn't intend to let anyone at the Valley of the Sun Inn get close enough to positively ID her.

Luckily, he didn't have to resort to any extraordinary measures. When he turned into the curving drive that led to the front entrance of the exclusive hotel and golf resort, he found it clogged by a fleet of the hotel's minibuses disgorging conventioners in golf shirts and shorts. From the chorus of the raucous male laughter, the businessmen had scored more booze than birdies that day.

That suited Marsh just fine. So did the harried expression the valet parking attendant wore as he wove through the throng to get to the Blazer. Marsh lowered the darkened driver's window just enough for the attendant to see his face. The tint on the other windows kept the Blazer's interior in shadows.

"Checking in, sir?"

"No. I'm checking to see if the owner is on the premises tonight."

"Mr. Jannisek? I don't think so. I just came on

an hour ago, but someone said he hasn't been around for a few days.''

Marsh had his badge ready. The kid's eyes widened when he caught the glint of blue enamel on gold.

''Call the front desk. Tell them Special Agent Henderson from the DEA wants to talk to Jannisek. If he's not here, I want to know where he is.'' He indicated his passenger with a little jerk of his head. ''So does Miss Smith.''

The valet stooped lower, his eyes widening.

''Becky? Hey, where have you...?''

Marsh made sure he got a glimpse—only a glimpse—before cutting him off with a brusque order.

''Move it! We're in an exposed position here.''

''Huh?''

''Make the call, kid. Now!''

''Yes, sir!''

The window whirred up. Marsh waited, his pulse hammering, for the woman beside him to break the sudden silence.

''That....'' She wet her lips and started again. ''That doesn't prove anything. He didn't really see me.''

''He saw enough to recognize you.''

She shook her head.

Even in the dim light filtering through the tinted windows, her hair gleamed a rich auburn. Marsh had known that tumble of burnt cinnamon would tag her. Had counted on it.

"He saw just what you wanted him to see," she said slowly.

The shrewd guess surprised him. So did the question she threw at him next.

"You *wanted* him to think I was Becky, didn't you?"

It hadn't taken her long to figure that one out. Marsh shifted in his seat, ready to deny the charge. He'd do whatever was necessary to bring down Ellen's killers. He'd already decided that. Already put himself over the line and made this pursuit his personal crusade. He was damned if he would offer either excuses or explanations.

He didn't have to. She came up with the explanation on her own.

"You don't really care *who* I am, do you?" Anger spiraled through her voice. "One sister will serve your purpose as well as the other, as long as David Jannisek doesn't know which one you have."

"Look, Becky or Lauren or whoever…"

"The name's Lauren, and *you* look!" She turned to him, twisting in her seat far as the seat belt would allow. "I decided back there at the house to go along with you because I love my sister and thought it was safer for her to stay hidden while I drew the dogs off her scent. If I find you've lied to me about this—about any of this—if you're just stringing me along for some perverted purpose of your own, I swear I'll…I'll…"

Her sputtering fury almost convinced him she was who she said she was. She looked so indignant, sounded so fierce, that if the valet hadn't come running back at that moment, Marsh might have abandoned his plan completely. Or at least, revised it yet again.

"Mr. Jannisek's not here," the kid panted. "But the hotel phone operator said he called the lounge a little while ago, looking for Becky, uh, Miss Smith." He bent down, craning to see the woman in the passenger seat. "She said he was real anxious to talk to you."

"Did he leave a number?"

The question jerked the valet's attention back to the driver. "No."

"Dammit."

Marsh slammed the wheel with a hard palm. They'd missed establishing contact with Jannisek by minutes. Mere minutes. Yanking open the glove compartment in the Blazer's dash, he shoved aside his spare ammo clip and cellphone to dig out the notepad he never went anywhere without.

"Here." Scribbling fast, he tore off a ragged-edged sheet and handed it to the valet. "Give this number to the hotel operators and tell them to pass it to Mr. Jannisek if he calls again asking for Miss Smith."

"Yeah, sure." The young man bobbed lower. "Anything you want me to tell him, Beck…?"

The window whirred, cutting off the question. Marsh shoved the Blazer into reverse.

Silence sizzled through the truck's interior during the drive out of the city. Within minutes, the signs for Interstate 17 flashed in the headlights. Marsh didn't breathe easy until the lights of Phoenix blurred in the rearview mirror.

He'd half expected the woman he now thought of as Becky-slash-Lauren to jump out of the truck at a red light or stop sign. He would've gone after her, of course, but slapping on a pair of cuffs and dragging her kicking and screaming back into the Blazer wouldn't exactly win him any points with her, much less win her cooperation for the next phase of his plan.

The possibility that such rough-and-ready tactics might also land him in the middle of a lawsuit for a violation of civil rights when this was all over was a risk he was willing to take. He'd already accepted that he could lose his badge for operating like this outside the parameters of his authority. When his brother Evan had heard that Marsh had decided to pick up the search for Ellen's killers where the locals had left off, the assistant D.A. had warned bluntly that Marsh was skating too close to the edge. So had his partner, Pepper Dennis.

He'd better call Pepper, Marsh thought as he downshifted to take the Blazer up the steep inclines of the mountains that ringed the valley. Alert her to the fact that Jannisek might try to check up on him, or discover just why the heck his girlfriend was now in the company of a DEA special agent.

Pepper would cover for him. She was a good agent, one of the best. Marsh had trained her himself. Although she wasn't particularly happy about the fact that her partner had put himself on indefinite leave or that he was operating without backup or official sanction, she understood why he had to see this thing through to the end. No matter how long it took.

And it might not take as long as he'd feared, Marsh thought, on a spike of pure adrenaline. He'd just received confirmation that Jannisek was alive and looking for his girlfriend. With a little luck and the right pressure, he could lure the man out of hiding and into custody within a few days, a week at most. His heart pumped pure adrenaline at the prospect of bringing Jannisek in.

To do that, though, he'd need at least a show of cooperation from the woman beside him. He slanted her a quick glance. Her rigid posture and stony profile scraped some of the edge off his anticipation.

The next phase might just prove the most difficult step in his plan. Funny, he'd thought it would be the easiest. He'd figured she'd be shaken by a seeming break-in—counted on her feeling isolated and helpless after being whisked away from her usual support systems. In his experience, most victims fell all over their rescuers in relief and gratitude.

Particularly a woman like Becky Smith, a sexy, kittenish flirt with more air than brains under that mass of silky auburn hair.

He gave her another sideways look. If this woman *was* Becky, she had proved that even the most detailed reports sometimes erred. She was no airhead, and she had more grit than anyone gave her credit for. She hadn't hesitated to grab a garbage can lid instead of running for cover back there at the house. Nor had she been shy about challenging his authority. After doing his damnedest to shake her up, Marsh hadn't expected her to stand toe to toe with him and demand to see his badge.

Maybe she really was this other sister, Lauren. Her passionate speech a few minutes ago about wanting to protect Becky had rung with angry sincerity.

Yet...

Like a video replaying in his mind, he pictured Becky Smith's cluttered living room, saw again the lace-trimmed scrap of violet silk on the floor. Saw, too, the sexy little smile she'd turned on like a light switch. She'd practically purred when she asked if he was wondering how her undies had ended up on the living room floor.

He'd wondered, all right. Okay, he'd done more than wonder. For a few seconds there, his imagination had pulled out all the stops. The tantalizing image of Becky Smith—or the woman he'd thought was Becky Smith—in the high-hipped lavender silk and nothing else had done a serious number on his respiratory system.

Just remembering that image, his chest got tight again. With some effort, Marsh banished the erotic picture. He intended to win Becky Smith's reluctant cooperation, not let her seduce him with those mile-long legs and perfect, pouty lips.

Unless he had to.

The thought slammed out of the darkness, hitting him like a fist to the jaw. For two, maybe three seconds, it raced around Marsh's head before he shoved it out.

No! No way he was going there. Getting cozy with another man's mistress went too far over the line, even for someone as determined as Marsh. If she *was* Jannisek's mistress. Like a dog chasing its tail, his thoughts made another frustrated circle.

Dammit, which sister was she? The uncertainty irritated Marsh, despite the fact that he'd already decided to proceed regardless of which Smith he'd pulled into his plan. It didn't matter, he reminded himself, as long as Jannisek didn't know who was talking to him on the other end of the phone line. Assuming Marsh could convince her to talk at all.

He might as well begin the convincing process by breaking the taut silence. A rustle of fabric as she rubbed her forearms provided an opening. Belatedly, he realized that the temperature had dropped a good ten degrees since they'd left Phoenix's desert environment behind and started the climb to the higher elevations of north-central Arizona.

"Are you cold?"

Still stiff, still obviously angry, she nodded. "A little."

"I'll turn on some heat, but I better warn you the thermostat's out of whack."

Since he rarely used the heater, even during El Paso's occasional blasts of frigid winter, Marsh hadn't bothered to get the thermostat adjusted after a wild chase through the Texas scrub. The chase had knocked the hell out of the Blazer and, in the process, netted two scum-sucking drug smugglers and three hundred kilos of uncut cocaine.

The stifling hot air that blasted out of the vents when he flicked the switch made him regret his lapse. Grimacing, he prepared to sweat. Scant minutes later, his passenger swiped her palms along her temples.

"I'm suffocating. Turn it off."

No please. No thank you. No kiss my left foot. Miss Smith was definitely ticked off.

"I've got an extra jacket in the back seat. You'd better put it on."

She shook her head, her eyes on the road ahead.

Marsh curled his fingers around the wheel. Nursing a sneezing, runny-nosed female through a cold didn't constitute part of his plan.

"Put on the jacket. There's a first-aid kit at the cabin, but I doubt if it contains any cold remedies."

"Cabin?" She lowered those winged brows, suspicion sharp in her voice. "I thought you said we were going to a ranch."

"We're going to a line cabin *on* a ranch. It's up in the foothills, at almost six thousand feet. That's why I brought a jacket along for you. You'll need it."

Reluctant but shivering again, she stretched around to reach between the seats for the flannel-lined suede jacket Marsh had tossed in at the last minute. The movement brought her head to within a few inches of his. To his disgust, he found himself holding his breath to keep from drawing in her seductive scent.

Great! They'd spent all of an hour together, and he was already steeling himself against her impact on his senses. The next few days could prove a real test of nerves for both of them.

"How long have you been seeing David Jannisek?" he asked, determined to keep his focus on his purpose—his only purpose—for drawing her into his scheme.

"How long has *my sister* been seeing him, you mean?" She shoved one arm into a jacket sleeve and groped behind her for the other. "You're the one who's been checking up on her. You tell me."

So they were going to play it the hard way. Fine. Marsh had broken far tougher prospects than this one in his time.

"From all reports, Jannisek and Becky Smith have been an item for about four months," he replied evenly, reaching over to help her into the jacket. "The same sources indicate he fell a lot harder than she did."

"If you say so."

"You may not see any reason to cooperate right now," he said softly, "but it's in your best interests to tell me everything you know about David Jannisek. Either firsthand or from your sister," he tacked on, as a concession to her insistence that she wasn't Becky.

"Why? You've got what you wanted. Bait for your trap. What more do you need?"

"A good hunter always knows his prey. I want every detail you can tell me about this guy. Things only a lover might know. His favorite dessert. The last movie you watched together. Hopes or plans or little wishes he might have let drop in bed."

"Even if I *was* Becky, do you think I would tell you intimate secrets like that?"

"You would if you wanted to save his hide," Marsh fired back. "The mob boss Jannisek owes big time to has already tried to gun him down once, remember?"

That took some of the starch from her spine. Slumping down in her seat, she tucked her hands under her arms and stared out at the narrow slice of landscape illuminated by the headlights. It had changed considerably during their journey.

Southern Arizona's fat saguaros and curly creosote bushes had already given way to mesquite and scrub pine. Soon, Marsh knew from so many drives along this route, the land would rise into the wind-sculpted red rock mesas surrounding Sedona. After that came the mountains, with their stands of aspen, blue spruce and ponderosa pine. They were only an hour away from their destination, maybe less. Once again he was heading home.

Only this time, Ellen wouldn't be there to welcome him back to the Bar-H, her arm wrapped around Jake's waist, and her shy smile lighting her eyes.

Marsh's gut tightened.

"What if I can't remember anything?"

The subdued question came out of the darkness.
He forced himself to relax. Was she finally going to
admit the truth? That he had, in fact, pulled the right
sister into his net?

No such luck.

"We talked about Dave Jannisek," she confessed.
"My sister and I. But..." Her hand lifted to spear
through her hair. "Becky falls in and out of love so
easily, I didn't pay a lot of attention to the details."

That was the understatement of the century. The
report on Becky Smith's past liaisons had read like
a soap opera magazine. Well, Marsh was willing to
take whatever crumbs he could get.

"I'll help you," he promised. "Sooner or later,
the details will come back."

"Sooner or later?" She tested the words, turning
her head toward his. Her brown eyes were unread-
able in the darkness. "Does it make a difference
which?"

"Not to me."

Chapter 5

"We're here."

Henderson's deep voice brought Lauren out of a semi-stupor induced by her two flights that day, long stretches of unbroken silence, and mile after mile of empty road.

She blinked owlishly and glanced at the clock on the dash, surprised to find that it was well after midnight. Sitting up, she searched the thick pines surrounding the car. If there was a cabin anywhere out there, she sure couldn't see it.

"Here where?"

"This is as far as the road goes."

He shouldered open his door, letting in a slice of cold air that nipped at Lauren's lungs. Her nose burrowed deeper into the collar of her borrowed jacket as she climbed out. She'd gotten used to its comforting combination of leather and flannel and spicy aftershave, with just a hint of horse thrown in for added fragrance. Once out of the Blazer, the sharp tang of pine resin added its scent to her still groggy senses.

"It's another fifty yards or so to the shack," Marsh announced as he dragged out her bag and his. "We walk from here."

"Hey, hold on a minute!"

"Is there a problem?"

"You tell me." Her breath pearling on the night air, Lauren faced him across the hood. "This place started off as a ranch. Then it morphed into a cabin *on* a ranch. Now it's a shack?"

"A line shack," he said with a touch of impatience. "Don't worry, it comes equipped with the necessary modern conveniences. Most of them, anyway."

Lauren didn't like the sound of that. She liked her first glimpse of the so-called cabin even less when it came into view a few moments later. Huffing from the cold and the uphill climb along a narrow dirt path, she took one look at the weathered structure and stopped in her tracks.

The building was tucked under a stand of pines. Enough moonlight filtered through the boughs to show the structure's rough-planked siding, corrugated tin roof and wraparound porch set off by split-log railings. Lauren was willing to concede that the place had a rustic sort of charm in the moonlight, but it definitely fell into the ''shack'' category.

No way around it. It was small. Too small for strangers to inhabit without tripping over each other on their way to the bathroom. If there was a bathroom....

That fear was laid to rest when they stepped inside and Marsh dumped the bags to light the oil lamp left on a convenient shelf beside the door. The flickering light soon illuminated a sort of kitchen/living room, dominated by a massive stone fireplace, with a door leading to a shadowy bunk room beyond. Handcrafted split-log furniture offered no-frills, man-sized comfort.

To Lauren's relief, another door at the rear of the kitchen revealed a gleam of porcelain. At least the place had indoor bathroom fixtures. Her moment of giddy relief evaporated when she poked her head inside the bunk room, however. It was just that—a room filled with bunks topped by bare mattresses. Folded sheets and blankets were stacked on a make-shift dresser. A squat, pot-bellied woodstove occupied the center space, alongside a table littered with poker chips and a deck of greasy-looking cards. A grossly overendowed Miss January 1987 provided the only decoration.

Pulling in a deep breath, Lauren backed out and took another survey of the main room. Her gaze went to the sofa, cushioned in red and dun cowhide, and then to Marsh.

''That better open into a bed for you or we're out of here. Now.''

Only after she'd issued the ultimatum did she stop to wonder how the heck she'd enforce it. The same thought must have occurred to Marsh. He flicked her a sardonic glance, but answered equably enough.

''It doesn't, but I've racked out on it before. I'll survive.''

''The DEA sends you up here often, does it?''

He answered with a shrug and passed her the tote and gym bag. ''You can get settled while I crank up the generator and haul in some wood.''

Moments later, the overhead light in the kitchen flickered on. Lauren found the switch for the bunk room and flooded the room with light. It didn't look any better than it had by the glow of the oil lamp.

Unpacking the few items she'd brought with her took all of three minutes. The jeans and tops went on pegs pounded into the wall. The sneakers she lined up beside the bunk closest to the stove. Becky's undies she left in the gym bag. She had her bed made and had strolled back into the main room by the time Marsh returned, his arms laden.

His boots echoed hollowly on the pine floorboards as he crossed to the fireplace and hunkered down. Within a remarkably short space of time, the kindling had fired a cheerful little blaze. Lauren was standing in the middle of the room, wondering what the heck she'd gotten herself into, when he pushed to his feet.

Tugging off his hat, he hooked it on the antlers

rack over the fireplace and shagged a hand through his hair. A black brow cocked as he took in her uneasy stance.

"Having second thoughts?"

"Second, third and fourth."

"About this place, or about coming with me?"

"Both."

Her glance went to the windows, as yet unshuttered to the night. The darkness beyond the wavy glass panes defied penetration. No lights winked in the distance. No beams of headlights cut through the pines. Lauren felt as though she and Marsh Henderson had dropped off the edge of civilization.

"In the movies the cops always whisk the star witness off to a hotel room or a safe house in another city. Not to an isolated mountain shack."

"This isn't a movie." A muscle ticked at the side of his jaw. "Those were real bullets aimed at Jannisek."

Lauren shivered under her blanket of suede. "And you really think you can lure him out of hiding despite the fact that more bullets might come zinging at him?"

"Not me." His lake-cool baby blues didn't reflect even a shadow of remorse. "You. When he calls around looking for Becky again, he'll get the word that I have her."

Lauren didn't particularly care for his word choice. Or for the prospect of being dangled like a piece prime beef in front of a desperately hungry man.

"What if he doesn't call anytime soon?"

"I've already told you, it doesn't matter how long this takes. I'm in this for the duration, Beck…"

"Lauren," she interjected. "The name's Lauren."

A flicker of annoyance crossed his face, as if the mix-up in identities were somehow her fault.

"Say it," she demanded.

His head inclined an inch, maybe less. "Lauren."

The victory was a small one, but she savored it until the tiredness dragging at her limbs convinced her that she couldn't go another round tonight.

"Well, we're here now and I'm wiped. We'll talk about the duration tomorrow. Do you want first dibs on the bathroom?"

"No, it's all yours. But you might want to wait until morning to take a shower. It'll take a few hours for the water to heat."

Lauren didn't waste time in the tiny bathroom. It was as cold as a refrigerator and just about the same size. Her skin was tingling from a quick splashing when she retreated to the bunk room and closed the door firmly behind her.

Marsh had gotten a fire started in the pot-bellied stove, thank goodness. Resin popped as the flames licked greedily at the iron grate, and the stove's warmth supplemented the weak glow put out by the space heater at the far end of the room.

Sagging onto the end of her bunk, Lauren huddled as close as she could get to the stove. Miss January smirked down at her from the opposite wall, her superabundance of naked flesh impervious to the chill.

This was wonderful, Lauren thought, morosely. Just wonderful. Not only had she exchanged her airy Denver bedroom with its spectacular views of the mountains for this cold little box of a shack, she was now sharing her quarters with 1987's queen of male fantasies.

And with a man she'd only met a few hours ago.

She was honest enough to admit that the idea of spending an indeterminate length of time in Marsh Henderson's company disturbed her almost as much as anything else in this bizarre situation. In the few short hours since she'd flown out the back door of Becky's house and into his arms, he'd taken Lauren down a fast track from gratitude to suspicion to fury. From the way her pulse had zinged all over the place when he'd laid that roguish grin on her, she suspected he could take her down a few other tracks if she'd let him.

"Not in this lifetime," she vowed to the skeptical Miss January.

Henderson had showed Lauren his true colors tonight. He might claim to be one of the good guys, but he was every bit as ruthless as the man he was hunting.

Dragging her tote across the bunk, she fished inside for her cellphone. Becky probably hadn't made it to Aunt Jane's yet, but Lauren could alert her that she was coming. The flashing message on the digital display killed that notion.

No service. Out of range.
No service. Out of range.
Wonderful!

Her mouth twisting, Lauren realized the phone salesman might have known what he was talking about when he'd advised her to shell out a few more dollars for a more powerful unit with nationwide coverage. With her business still long on potential and short on cash flow, she'd opted for the cheaper, urban-area service instead. Now she was paying the hidden costs he'd tried to warn her about.

She rubbed the heel of her hand against her forehead, fighting the tiredness that pulled at her. How in the heck would she contact Becky?

Henderson had brought a phone. She'd glimpsed it in the car, and again when he'd dumped his gear in the living room. She knew his would work, even out here in the wilds—anxious as he was for David Jannisek to contact him.

Now all she'd have to do was figure out a way to separate Henderson from his phone. She'd work on that problem tomorrow, she decided. She was fast reaching the overload point tonight.

Bracing herself for the cold, Lauren got ready for bed. Her stacked heel shoes hit the floor with a thump. The jeans followed a moment later. Goose bumps popped out on her thighs and stomach as she forced herself to shed the suede jacket, her stretchy knit top and sensible, comfortable *un*-wired bra. Shivering, she dove into the Arizona Suns T-shirt she'd snatched from the pile of clean laundry on her sister's floor. Only then did she discover that Becky had scissored the shirt to bust-skimming length. The darned thing left more midriff bare than it covered.

The clean undies she dragged out of the gym bag covered even less. Cursing her sister's predilection for minimal clothing and maximum exposure, Lauren wiggled the panties into place. The thong rubbed against her with all the comfort of Number Three fishing line as she yanked another blanket off the shelf.

A quick side trip doused the lights. With only the glow from the stove to guide her, she spread the blanket and crawled into the bunk, yelping out loud when her bare skin hit icy sheets.

On the other side of the thin wall that separated the bunk area from the bathroom, Marsh heard a strangled cry over the splash of running water.

His head shot up. Soapy cold water ran from his face onto his neck and bare chest. His brain processed the sound in two seconds flat. His feet were moving in three. Instincts honed by more than a decade working undercover had his Glock cocked and his boot against the bunk-room door in another ten.

The door crashed against the wall.

Marsh charged in.

The woman in the bunk closest to the glowing woodstove bolted upright. Thrusting a pile of blankets away from her face, she took one look at his two-fisted stance and shrieked again. Her screech was still bouncing off the walls when she kicked at the tangled blankets, lost her balance, and tumbled off the narrow bunk.

Pulse pounding, body in an instinctive half crouch, Marsh spun a full 360 degrees and searched for the cause of Becky's distress. Lauren's distress. Whoever!

In the reddish glow from the stove, he registered the room's one closed window, its glass unbroken. The rest of the beds unmade and undisturbed. Miss January in the same provocative pose she'd held since one of his brothers had reverently pinned her in place more than a decade ago. But nothing to raise a cry of alarm.

He hit the wall switch, and did another search. Still nothing.

Blowing out a ragged breath, he uncocked the weapon and laid it aside before stepping over to the thrashing bundle of blankets to grasp Becky's arm. Lauren's arm. Dammit, *her* arm. Pumping adrenaline and a surge of sheer annoyance at not knowing whose soft flesh he grasped put a sharp edge to his voice.

"Are you okay?"

"I was until you burst in!"

She scrambled up in a welter of scratchy wool blankets and tumbled hair, giving him a view of the sorriest excuse for a T-shirt he'd ever seen. When Marsh saw what she *wasn't* wearing below that scrap of cotton, his stomach kicked clear back to his spine.

"What's…what's wrong?" Panting, she dug her

fingers into his arm to steady herself. "Why did you storm in like that?"

With a Herculean effort, he dragged his gaze from the expanse of bare, quivering skin above her belly button.

"I heard a scream."

"A scream?" Her voice spiraled upward. It didn't take his decade of undercover experience to see she was still as pumped as he was. "Who screamed?"

"You, I thought."

"I didn't make a sou...! Oh."

She released her death grip, leaving nail marks in his arms, and shoved back her hair. The movement dragged the shirt up.

Marsh swallowed. Hard.

"Well, maybe I did let out a little gasp when I climbed into bed."

"Gasp, hell! I heard you right through the wall. Why did you screech like that?"

"I did not screech. I merely—squawked."

"Care to explain why?"

"The sheets were cold. They felt like ice."

What the Sam Dickens did she expect, given the amount of exposed skin available to make contact with the blasted sheets? Exercising considerable restraint, Marsh refrained from pointing out the obvious. His restraint didn't extend to denying himself another quick sweep of bare stomach, trim flanks and long, luscious legs, however.

He was still taking in the view when she bent to

retrieve the blankets and gave him a glimpse of rounded bottom cheeks bisected by a T-strap.

He broke out in a sweat.

"You scared the heck out of me," she grumbled, still rattled and not happy about it.

"Sorry."

He backed away, retrieving the Glock on his way to the door. He had to get out of there before he did something monumentally stupid—like giving her time to notice the fact that he wasn't breathing.

"Go to sleep."

"I intend to," she muttered, dumping the blankets on the bunk. "As soon as my heart stops jumping."

Marsh's heart performed a few jumps of it own as she yanked the bed coverings into place and crawled in. She was still twitching the pillow into position when he doused the lights and beat a hasty retreat. He didn't pull in a whole breath until he reentered the bathroom he'd raced out of scant moments before.

It didn't surprise him that the face staring back at him from the square shaving mirror tacked above the sink showed skin flushed and taut across the cheekbones. Just thinking about the woman who'd floundered free of her blankets got him hot above the waist and hard below. Lord! Did the woman have any idea of what she did to a man's nervous system?

If she was Becky Smith, she did.

That thought cooled him off faster than the icy

water he slapped on his face to wash off the drying soap.

If she was Becky Smith, she knew exactly what impact those long legs and curving flanks would have on him. The same impact they'd had on half a dozen other men at various times during the past year—including David Jannisek. Becky had racked up more trophies than a world-class champion bull rider.

And what about the sister? What if she *was* Lauren Smith, as she claimed? Did she collect trophies with the same effortless ease as her sister?

In another time, under other circumstances, Marsh might not have objected to being collected by the woman in the next room. Wouldn't have objected, either, to exploring her mouth with his tongue, and her enticing rear with his palms. But he hadn't brought her up here to play games with her.

Besides, those kind of games could get in the way of his plan. Jannisek had already called once looking for his girlfriend. He'd call again, sooner or later. Marsh would stick to his game plan, draw the man in, go over or around or through him to get to El-len's killers. He'd convince Becky to cooperate—or Lauren to cooperate by acting as Becky.

Dammit, which one was she? Frustration nipped at him again as he toweled off and shagged his shirt from the john seat. He didn't like this uncertainty. Didn't like not having the edge of knowing who the heck he was dealing with. Hopefully, Pepper would have a positive ID for him tomorrow. In the meantime, he'd better push the image of Ms. Smith's all-too-sexy posterior out of his mind or he'd never get any sleep.

He woke the next morning to a stiff neck, a rumbling stomach, and the annoying awareness that putting Becky/Lauren out of his mind and keeping her out were two different matters. For the first time since he'd decided to go after Jannisek, he felt a twinge of sympathy for his prey.

From all reports, the hotelier had gone off the deep end for the cocktail waitress who might or might not be tucked up in the bunk room. She'd gotten under his skin, according to all accounts, like an itch that required continual scratching. Marsh would just make damned sure she didn't get under his.

That resolution stayed firmly in his mind as he rolled off the lumpy cowhide-covered cushions, while he pulled a clean shirt and shaving kit from his gear bag, during his shower, and as he put the coffee on. It got shot all to hell when the bunk-room door opened fifteen minutes later.

A good inch of bacon grease sizzled in the cast-iron skillet in which Big John had taught his boys to fry everything from eggs to venison. Marsh had just transferred a thick slab of bacon onto a plate and was forking another into the hot grease when he heard her shuffle out of the bunk room. He paused in his task long enough to toss a casual good morning over his shoulder.

"What's so good about it?" she grumbled as she padded toward the bathroom, an embroidered toiletries bag in hand.

"Not a morning person, huh?"

"Not any kind of a person until I inject some caffeine into my system."

"The coffee's ready if you want to pour yourself a mug."

She grunted and detoured into the kitchen long enough to fill one of the chipped mugs. The bathroom door banged shut behind her a moment later, leaving Marsh with hot grease spitting against his hand and a grin pulling at his mouth.

In the dark of night this woman had come flying out of a back door and crashed into him, all long limbs and dangerous curves. That combination had proved disturbing enough, but it didn't compare to the erotic image of the same woman in half a T-shirt and a few strategically placed strings that had kept him awake most of the night.

Given the choice, he knew darned well he'd vote for the thong anytime. Yet, he found himself curiously impatient for this sleepy-eyed grump in jeans, sneakers and an oversized sweatshirt to emerge from the bathroom.

Chapter 6

Feeling less than happy with the world in general
and with a certain DEA agent in particular, Lauren
rubbed a clear spot in the steamed-up bathroom mirror. A decidedly unimpressive reflection glared back
at her. Wet hair straggled down her neck. Her skin
glowed brick red from the hot shower—everywhere
that wasn't pimpled white by the nippy morning air,
that is. She looked like a walking disaster, which
was exactly how she felt.

What in the world was she doing in this tiny
cabin, somewhere in the wilds of northern Arizona?
More to the point, how the heck was she going to
get through an indeterminate number of hours with
only Marsh Henderson and a bunch of pine trees for
company?

The man disturbed her.

Ha! Who was she kidding? He disturbed, infuriated and still frightened her just a little. In the cold light of day, his plan to set Becky up as bait seemed even more ruthless than it had last night. Nor would she forgive him anytime soon for his callous decision to substitute one sister for another. And that gun! Even after a restless night spent on a mattress that didn't in any way measure up to box-spring standards, the memory of Marsh bursting through the bunk-room door with that evil-looking weapon in his hands sent her mind skittering in a dozen different directions.

Shivering, she tucked the man-sized towel tighter under her arms, and then squeezed toothpaste onto her brush and attacked her teeth. She could still see him in that half crouch, muscles corded, danger radiating from him in almost palpable waves. He'd scared her half out of her wits. She could just imagine his impact on Becky. Her sister would have died. Or melted all over the guy.

The toothbrush stilled. Fluoride-flavored foam bubbled in Lauren's mouth. Scowling, she forced the drippy face in the mirror to 'fess up.

Okay. All right. She could admit it. For a second or two last night, she'd felt an irrational urge to melt all over the guy, too. Not that she would ever do it. The crazy impulse was just a reaction to all that raw, masculine power. And to the fact that Marsh had burst in to rescue her. Only from a set of icy sheets, of course, but he hadn't known that at the time.

Disgusted with the path her wayward thoughts had taken, Lauren spit out the toothpaste and rinsed her mouth. She had to get real here—remember who he was and why he'd brought her to this isolated cabin. She was a means to an end. Period. End of story.

Somehow, that didn't make her feel any better. Nor did the fact that she'd forgotten some absolute essentials in her hurried departure from Becky's house last night—like a hairbrush, a blow-dryer and a curling iron, to mention just a few.

Grimacing, she dragged a comb through wet tangles that would eventually dry to an unruly mass of red. On Becky, the natural look meant long, bouncy curls. On Lauren, natural translated to Little Orphan Annie after a close encounter with an electrical socket.

She gave up after a couple more passes with the comb and took a slug of her now cooling coffee. The chicory-flavored brew had the consistency of axle grease, but acted like a cattle prod on her senses. By the time she finished slapping on a minimum of makeup, she felt ready for her next encounter with Marsh Henderson. It wouldn't, she suspected, be a particularly enjoyable experience. She'd done some hard thinking after he'd backed out and left her staring at the bunk-room door last night.

He was waiting for her when she emerged from the bathroom. Mug in hand, he sprawled at ease in one of the sturdy kitchen chairs drawn up to the scrubbed pine table. A covered cast-iron skillet sat on a horseshoe that doubled as a trivet. Beside it was a stack of toast. The coffeepot, thank goodness, occupied another horseshoe in the center of the table.

He took in her wildly curling hair without comment, although Lauren could swear his eyes widened for a moment before he leaned forward to lift the lid from the skillet.

"Hope you like your eggs fried."

She surveyed the heavily peppered whites and half-cooked yolks floating in a slowly congealing nest with something less than enthusiasm. A black-coffee-and-whole-wheat-bagel woman herself, she wasn't into grease.

"I'm not much of a breakfast eater. Just toast is enough for me."

"I'll remember that."

He said it so easily, as if they'd be sharing a number of morning meals. Her stomach lurching, she sank into the chair opposite his and helped herself to a single slice of toast burnt black around the edges and soggy with butter in the center.

They ate in silence. Lauren nibbled on her toast, and Marsh cleaned his plate with the healthy appetite of a man used to his own cooking. He was halfway through his eggs when she broached the subject that had kept her awake long after he'd backed out of the bunk room.

"I've been thinking about what you said last night—about cooperating."

"Good."

He raised his mug and took a triumphant swig. Lauren sensed the anticipation that leaped through him, the sudden tensing of his body. He was waiting for her to pour out everything she knew about David Jannisek. Unfortunately, she knew nothing to pour.

Not that Marsh would believe her. Until they settled this business of her identity, she occupied the hot seat. For that reason, Lauren had decided that the best defense was a good offense.

"I've also been thinking about your threat to haul me in front of a judge." She fiddled with a burnt crust for a moment, and then lifted her eyes to his. "I don't know much about the law, but I do know I have certain rights. I've decided to plead the fifth."

"What?"

"The Fifth Amendment. It's part of our Constitution," she pointed out with overdone politeness.

"Thanks for the civics lesson." His mug hit the table with a thunk. "You've been watching too much TV. You can't take the fifth. You haven't been indicted for a crime, nor are you testifying in a government proceeding."

"You work for the government. That's proceeding enough for me." Her chin tipped. "I refuse to incriminate myself or my sister."

"Oh, for...." He bit off what Lauren suspected was a nasty little curse and blew out a breath. "That business about the judge and hauling you off in handcuffs was nine parts bluff."

"Really? What about the tenth part?"

He leaned forward, shoving his mug aside. "The

offer of protective custody was for real. If the man who wants David Jannisek taken out is as anxious to find him as we are, Becky Smith could be in real danger.''

"Yet it didn't seem to matter much last night whether you took Becky or me into protective custody. All you wanted was something or someone to lure Jannisek out of hiding.''

A line of red appeared across his cheekbones. She had him there, Lauren knew. He couldn't deny his intent to use whichever sister he'd taken in tow.

He didn't even try. "The two goals are not mutually exclusive.''

The flat statement set her teeth on edge. "That's funny,'' she retorted. "In my book, offering someone protection and setting them up as bait don't fall into quite the same category.''

"I won't let anything happen to you. Or your sister.''

"How do I know that? How do I know you're not just determined to score some big coup or win a promotion by bringing down your quarry?'' Disdain dripped corrosively from her voice. "What's riding on this operation, an all-expense-paid trip to Disney World as a prize for the officer who nails this mobster?''

Marsh almost told her then. Almost gave in to the impulse to set her straight about just how much rode on this operation. The memory of Jake's stony grief held him back. Ellen's loss was too painful—and Marsh's own quest for vengeance too close to the line—to share it with a woman who might or might not be up to her pretty neck in the mess that had led to the vicious shooting.

"It doesn't matter why I want him," he said quietly. "All that matters is that I'm going to get him. But I won't put anyone in the line of fire to do it."

Except himself.

"You have my word on that."

He expected her to throw the promise back in his face. She looked as though she wanted to. Her lower lip was between her teeth again. A frown slanted those dark brows and formed a tiny crease just above her nose.

It was now or never, Marsh sensed. If he was going to regain her trust, convince her to abandon that ridiculous Fifth-Amendment stand and cooperate, he had to do it now. He dug into his hip pocket and extracted a set of keys.

"I won't hold you here against your will." The keys jingled as he dropped them on the table. "You can leave whenever you want. Or whenever you think it's safe for you…or your sister."

She stared at him for long moments before slumping back in her chair with a sigh. "I'm staying. Until I know it's safe for Becky to come out of hiding."

Marsh masked his relief by reaching for the coffeepot. He wasn't sure what the hell he would've done if she'd reached for those keys.

"Let's talk about what you know about our…"

The shrill ring of his cellular phone cut into the air. The coffeepot slammed down, sloshing a stream of dark liquid through its dented spout. Marsh ignored the spill, ignored too the startled gasp of the woman opposite him, and dug his phone out of his pocket.

Had the word gotten back to Jannisek already? Was he ready to deal? His pulse hammering, Marsh flipped up the cover and hit the talk button before the third ring.

"Henderson."

"Hey, partner. How's it going?"

Disappointment barreled through him. He fought it down, managed a nonchalant response.

"It's going."

Pepper Dennis had worked with him long enough to pick up instantly on his careful tone. "Is she there? The Smith woman?"

Marsh's gaze snagged on wide-spaced brown eyes flecked with tiny bits of gold. "Right here."

Pepper grunted an acknowledgment. "I ran the ID you gave me last night. The license checks out to Lauren Smith, but I couldn't raise an answer at her home or office. I finally got a line on her assistant. He wasn't exactly a fount of information at first, but I convinced him it was in his best interests to cooperate."

"So what did Ms. Smith's assistant tell you?"

The face across from his went still. He noted her sudden stiffening, felt his own muscles get tight as he waited for his partner to report her findings.

"Only that his boss was supposed to return from D.C. last night and has been delayed," Pepper related. "I had the guys upstairs run a data search of the airlines' manifests. They verified Lauren Smith flew in from D.C. to Denver, and then flew out again yesterday evening for Phoenix. She arrived about an hour before you called me. Looks like you've got the wrong sister."

He'd grown more and more convinced of that in the past twelve hours. Hearing it confirmed didn't exactly fill him with joy, however. Nor did Pepper's next comment.

"I'm sorry, Marsh. I know this screws up your plan. Maybe she can give you a lead on Becky-Babe's whereabouts before you send her on her way."

"She's not going anywhere."

"What?"

"She's staying here. For now, anyway."

The woman across the table followed his conversation intently, frowning beneath that wild tangle of red.

"You can't involve an innocent civilian like this," Pepper protested. "You'd better get her on the next plane out of Flagstaff."

"I know what I'm doing."

"Do you? I'm beginning to wonder. You're putting yourself out on a limb here, partner. Way out."

He brushed aside her concern. It was his career—and his sister-in-law who'd taken a bullet.

"Just keep the communication lines open, Pepper. Jannisek is looking for his girlfriend. He called the Valley of the Sun Inn last night looking for her. I made sure the folks there know Becky Smith is with a special agent of the DEA. Or the woman they think is Becky Smith.''

''Marsh…''

''Let me know if you hear anything. Anything at all.''

The phone flipped shut on Pepper's grudging agreement. He slipped the instrument into his shirt pocket and regarded the woman across from him.

''Well?''

''Well, Lauren Smith's license checks out, and we've confirmed that she was aboard a flight from Denver to Phoenix last night.''

''And…?''

''And you're apparently who you say you are.''

''And…?''

Marsh had grilled enough suspects to make them squirm. He didn't particularly like being on the other end of the grilling.

''And I suggest we clean up here and take a walk.'' He pushed away from the table. ''I need some fresh air.''

''Oh, no!'' She intercepted him before he'd taken two steps. ''You're not getting off that easy.''

Hands on hips, she tossed back the hair that had appeared so smooth and silky last night and now seemed to have taken on another life. ''I think an apology is in order here, Mr. Special Agent.''

''For wanting confirmation of your identity? I don't think so.''

''For not believing me in the first place.''

"Accepting people at face value isn't an option in my line of work."

"Maybe you should think about another line of work."

"Maybe I should."

He made to move around her. She sidestepped neatly.

"I'm waiting."

He could, he supposed, wrap his hands around her waist and lift her out of the way. Or he could kiss that I-was-right-and-you-were-*so*-wrong expression off her mouth.

To his profound disgust, the mere idea translated instantly into a gut-level urge to do just that. With that wild mane and tip-tilted chin, she triggered all the wrong responses in him.

"All right. I'm sorry you went through some rough moments last night. Satisfied?"

She pursed her lips, considering the matter. "No, but I suppose that's the best I'll get."

Marsh tore his gaze from her seductive mouth. The air in the cabin seemed to have closed in on him. A walk in the woods sounded better and better.

"I'll clean up here. Get your jacket and I'll show you around."

"Fair is fair. You made breakfast. I'll help with the cleanup."

She reached for the skillet at the same moment he did. The brush of her arm against his was slight, a mere slide of a jersey sweatshirt against denim, yet his muscles jumped like live electrical wires.

"Just get your coat," he growled. "You can pull cleanup duty at lunch."

She wheeled away without another word, leaving Marsh feeling like ten kinds of a fool. This was absurd. He'd better get himself under control, like right now.

He should have expected his nerves to go on full alert at her touch. He'd spent half the night thinking about her. Analyzing her responses to his questions. Wondering which sister she was. Visualizing her in that damned thong. He'd imprinted her on his mind, the way a cougar imprinted the scent of its prey. Naturally he'd jump like a snake-shy mountain cat when she got too close.

Still frowning over her effect on him, he dumped the skillet in the sink and fished the phone out of his pocket again. He had put off this call as long as possible. Might as well get it over with now.

After months of constant communication with the Phoenix detective investigating Ellen's death, Marsh recognized the strain in Al Ramos's voice the moment he picked up. Ramos was a good man, but overworked like everyone else on the force. Marsh was about to complicate his life considerably.

"This is Henderson. I've got Becky Smith—or the woman everyone now thinks is Becky Smith."

"The hell you say!"

"She showed up at her house last night."

"Dammit, Henderson, you should have contacted me."

"I'm contacting you now."

Ramos gave that the response it deserved. Marsh barely had time to admire his inventive use of the idiom before the detective zeroed in on his opening statement.

"What's this business about everyone *thinking* she's Becky Smith?"

"Our little bird's holed up somewhere. Her sister came looking for her last night."

"So you snatched *her?*" Incredulity laced the detective's voice. "The sister?"

"She agreed to come with me."

"Sure she did." After a few more colorful invectives, he sang a now familiar chorus. "God, Henderson, you don't have any jurisdiction in this case."

"I know."

"You get in any deeper and even your hot-shot assistant D.A. brother won't be able to dig you out."

"I'm not asking him to."

Ramos fired off a few more heated rounds before getting to the matter that concerned them both.

"Does the woman with you know where Jannisek is?"

"She says she doesn't. But she does know where her sister is. She swears Becky's not with her boyfriend."

"And you believe her?"

Marsh gazed through the window over the sink at dark pines spearing a cloudless blue sky. Did he believe her?

"At this point, I don't have any choice."

"So what are you going to do now?" Ramos asked with heavy irony. "Use a rubber hose to beat her sister's whereabouts out of her?"

"It's a thought. A very interesting thought. But no, I'm sticking to my original plan."

Swiftly, he brought Ramos up to speed on their short detour by the Valley of the Sun Inn.

"Work your contacts, will you, Al? Make sure the word gets out that I have Becky Smith."

"You're gonna get my ass fired with this crazy plan," the detective muttered.

"You got a better one?"

The grudging silence at the other end of the line served as his answer. He hung up a moment later and turned to find Becky—Lauren—staring at him from the across the room.

"Who was that?"

"The detective in charge of investigating the attempt on Jannisek's life."

"I thought you were in charge."

"I'm assisting," he replied without batting an eye. "Come on, I'll show you around. I don't want you wandering off and getting lost. We're a long way from nowhere."

Chapter 7

Dazzling light surrounded Lauren the moment she stepped outside. Stunned by a sense of vastness and seduced by the sharp, cleansing air, she quickly amended the hazy impressions she'd gathered last night. This morning, her artist's eye saw the cabin as less of a shack and more like a tiny gem in a perfect, jeweled setting.

Nestled within the protection of tall pines, it faced out over a small clearing. The shack's weathered siding gleamed the same silvery gray as the fallen logs that littered the clearing. The hand-hewn porch rails were of native timber, planed to a silky smoothness. Lauren knew little about architecture and nothing at all about log-cabin construction, but even she could see that the structure had been crafted by a master hand to blend in perfectly with its environment.

But it was the view from the front porch that took her breath away. Evidently they'd driven higher into the mountains last night than she'd realized. Beyond the small clearing, the trees dropped away with startling suddenness. From where she stood, she could see for miles.

The tiny cabin seemed to hover halfway between the sky and the wide, meandering valley far below. The steep slopes were carpeted with verdant spruce and pine. Aspens just tipped with the first touch of fall color cascaded like ribbons of gold against the darker evergreens. Stands of new growth where loggers had replanted harvested areas spread like blankets of pale green.

The small clearing in front of the cabin had gone to tall grasses and a riot of gold, violet and red wildflowers. It was an idyllic setting, both calm and uplifting at the same time—or at least that's how Lauren perceived it until she stepped off the porch and caught sight of the snow-capped peaks behind the cabin. They stood tall and jagged against the sky, like glistening teeth ready to tear into anyone or anything foolish enough to come within their reach.

"What mountains are those?"

Settling his black Stetson low on his forehead, Marsh gave the rugged slopes a look of healthy respect.

"They're the San Franciscos." He leaned closer, pointing over her shoulder to one that reached higher into the sky than the others. "That's Humphreys Peak. At twelve-thousand-plus feet, it's the highest point in Arizona."

Suddenly, disturbingly conscious of the tanned cheek only inches from her own, Lauren half turned and shifted her field of vision to a volcanic cone rising from a black lava field across the valley.

"And that?"

"That's Sunset Crater. You'll see how it got its name later this afternoon, when that rim of orange ash and cinder starts to glow.

"If we're still here later this afternoon," she murmured.

She swung around, grazing his vest with her shoulder. They both stepped back, as if even that slight contact violated some unwritten ground rules for the duration of their stay.

"Do you really think David Jannisek will try to contact you today?"

His face took on a stony cast. "I'm hoping he will, but I can wait as long as it takes."

"So you said."

"What about you?" he asked, his eyes intent under the brim of his hat. "You said you wanted to protect your sister by drawing the dogs off her scent. How long are you prepared to act as decoy for Becky?"

The question hit Lauren right where she was most vulnerable these days—her fledgling business. Biting down on her lower lip, she wandered past him toward the edge of the clearing. Native grasses brushed at her calves. Bits of deadwood crunched under her sneakers.

It had taken her more than a year to recover from the financial disaster of her divorce, and another year to secure the loans to purchase the supplies and equipment to start up her own firm. Now, after months of long days and even longer nights in her studio, she was just starting to establish a toehold in the highly competitive note-card market.

Her stomach curled at the thought of the meeting she'd instructed Josh to cancel. The museum account might have taken her business out of the red for the first time. Then there were the prototype note cards for the Breckinridge Group. She'd planned to screen them in sepia tones to convey a sense of the hotel's long history and western tradition. The screens had to be done with a light touch or the artwork would wash out completely. Josh was a whiz on the computer, but he didn't have Lauren's eye or her training.

Marsh could hole up here indefinitely, but could she?

She didn't have to search very deep inside herself for the answer. Looking out for Becky came as natural as breathing to her. She'd rushed to her sister's rescue so many times, and drawn such comfort from Becky's irrepressible good humor, that everything else faded into insignificance in comparison to her safety.

Dragging in lungsful of sharp mountain air, she retraced her steps. Marsh stood where she'd left him.

Thumbs looped in his waistband, hat riding low on his forehead, he looked every bit as tough and unyielding as the mountains behind him.

"I'll play it one day at a time. If I decide to leave, you'll be the first to know."

He inclined his head an inch or two. "Fair enough."

"I'll need to use your phone later this morning. I have to contact my assistant."

"No problem. What about your sister?"

He slipped that in so casually that Lauren knew instantly she'd better reconsider last night's plan to keep in touch with Becky. She suspected that any call made from Marsh's phone to Aunt Jane would result in federal agents showing up at Jane's door within an hour. She wasn't ready to violate her sister's sanctuary.

"I told her to stay where she is until I contact her. I'll do that when I know it's safe."

His brow hitched. "You still don't trust me?"

"Would you?"

The skin at the sides of his eyes crinkled in the beginnings of a grin. "I don't trust anyone, sweetheart."

She was just gearing up to inform him that she didn't particularly appreciate sexist endearments like "sweetheart" or "honey" when he wrapped a hand around her elbow to help her over a patch of decaying deadwood.

The casual courtesy axed the rebuke she'd intended to deliver. There were certain aspects of chauvinism she appreciated, and she couldn't very well slam him for one and accept the other.

"I'll show you how to fuel the generator," he said. "Just in case."

"Just in case of what?" Alarmed, she dragged to a stop. "You're not thinking of going off and leaving me here alone, are you?"

"Of course not. But it doesn't hurt to be prepared for any contingency."

"Like what?"

"Like a tumble down a slope that could bust an arm or a rib," he offered with the casual unconcern of someone who'd experienced both. That sounded ominous enough to Lauren. The rider he then tacked on sounded even worse.

"Or an unexpected encounter with a black bear."

"You're kidding, right? You don't really expect us to go face-to-face with wild animals?"

"If we do, you just let out a screech like you did last night, and they'll go hightailing it for cover."

"I thought we'd already settled this. I did *not* screech. I merely yelped a little."

The grin that had started a few minutes ago appeared now in full force. "Could have fooled me."

If Lauren hadn't lived the past three years in mile-high Denver, she might have ascribed her sudden breathlessness to the thin air at this elevation. Since her lungs had long ago learned to extract every molecule of oxygen from the air around her, she couldn't use that flimsy excuse to explain the crazy kick in her respiratory system.

The root cause could only be Marsh's smile. It softened his rugged features and grooved the skin at the corners of his mouth. It also set off alarms all up and down Lauren's spine. She'd just told him that she didn't trust him, for heaven's sake! She'd better remember why.

"So where's this generator you want to show me?"

"Around back."

He hunkered down beside the humming unit some twenty or so yards from the cabin. Unlatching the door to its air-vented metal enclosure, he showed Lauren a surprisingly clean little motor topped by a bright-red fuel tank.

"This is a Honda 2000, one of the safest and most reliable units on the market. It'll run for forty-six hours on one tank of gas, or for twice that if you don't draw full power."

"Full power being the electric heaters, refrigerator and lights?"

"And the hot-water heater. This is the ignition switch. This is where you add the gas." A jerk of his chin indicated a small wooden storage shed a few yards away. "The gas is stored over there."

Balancing on one heel, Lauren gave the motor a thorough once over. It didn't look all that complicated, but she sincerely hoped they wouldn't have to depend on her mechanical skills to keep the lights on and the fridge running.

"Don't touch any engine parts while it's running," Marsh warned. "They get hot. Real hot.

Don't add fuel while it's running, and *never* light any matches or cigarettes around either the generator or the extra gasoline.''

"Don't touch, don't fuel, don't light. Got it."

When he was satisfied she understood the basics, Marsh relatched the door to the unit.

"I'm surprised you don't keep it under lock and key," she commented, noting the absence of a padlock in the hasp. "As small as it is, someone could cart the thing off."

"It wouldn't do a stranded hiker or a ranch hand caught by an early blizzard much good if they couldn't get at it."

"I didn't realize the DEA operated with such humanitarian concern for the common man."

"The DEA doesn't own this property," he replied, pushing to his feet. "We just use it on occasion."

His hand came down to help her up. It was another small courtesy, an unthinking one. Someone had hammered manners into this rough-edged cop. Or maybe they were instinctive. Lauren folded her hand into his, wondering for the first time about the man behind the shield.

He didn't wear a wedding ring, but many married men didn't, including her own gone-and-unregretted ex. Her curiosity piqued, Lauren tried to think of a subtle way to elicit a few details about her temporary companion. As they circled back to the front of the cabin, she finally decided on the direct approach.

"Do you do this often? Hole up with strange women for indefinite periods of time, I mean?"

"Not often."

"What does Mrs. Special Agent Henderson think about this aspect of your chosen profession?"

He slid her an amused glance. "There isn't a Mrs. Special Agent Henderson, if that's what you're asking."

It was, but Lauren saw no reason to say so.

"But if there was," he continued with a careless shrug, "she'd have to accept that situations like this come with the job."

"Boy, are you living in a dreamworld."

"You think?"

"Let me put it this way. When you find this paragon of patience and trust, you'd better grab her with both hands and never let go."

The amusement went out of his eyes. It was as if a curtain dropped, blanking out all thought and emotion.

"I'll remember that."

Uh-oh. She'd hit a nerve there. Lauren was still wondering which one when he tossed her question right back at her.

"What about you? You said you needed to call your assistant. Isn't there someone else you should notify about your extended stay in Arizona? Someone," he said, parroting her own query, "who might object to you holing up for an indefinite period with a strange man?"

"Not anymore."

To Lauren's considerable surprise, the admission had a strangely liberating effect. She felt no trace of the bitterness and hurt that had dogged her during the first months after the divorce. No lingering sense of betrayal. No disgust with herself for being so naive and trusting. Only a clean sensation of freedom.

It must be this sharp mountain air, she decided. It cut into her lungs and swept through her body, blowing away all the accumulated cobwebs. Or maybe it was the urgency of Becky's situation. The idea that mobsters might be searching for her sister left no room for petty, personal hurts.

Or it could be the man beside her, she admitted silently. From the moment she'd careened into him last night, he'd crowded almost everyone and everything else out of her mind.

No wonder. In a few short hours, he'd totally disrupted her life, her business and her preconceived notions of law enforcement officers. She never imagined they could be so ruthless—or so damned attractive.

She put the brakes on that thought, fast. Granted, Marsh Henderson looked even more dangerously handsome in the light of day than he had in the dark of night. And she'd bet he could tempt a postmenopausal nun to sin with one of his devastating grins if he put his mind to it. The fact that Lauren's own love life since her divorce bore remarkable similarity to the most devout nun's went a long way toward explaining why the heck her skin prickled whenever he cranked up a smile.

She'd darn well better remember he was here to lure another man into a trap, and she was here as bait. *Her* only purpose in accompanying Marsh to this mountain retreat was to protect her sister. She'd remind herself of that sobering fact every time her skin started to prickle.

With that resolve fixed firmly in her mind, Lauren followed while Marsh finished his guided tour of the cabin and its grounds. Other than the generator and fuel storage shed out back and the spectacular view out front, there wasn't much to see—until Marsh bent back a low bush and showed her a small, innocuous-looking metal disk.

"It's an infrared heat sensor," he explained. "I've strung a whole network around the cabin as a sort of perimeter defense."

"Defense against what?" she asked, startled.

"Unannounced visitors."

The casual reply was hardly reassuring.

"It's a relatively simple alarm system, but the sensors are sophisticated enough to distinguish the body temperature of an animal from that of a human. The old ones used to go off every time a raccoon ambled by."

Unsure whether she should feel reassured or trapped by the electronic fence, Lauren led the way back inside.

"So what do we do now?" she asked, when the door shut behind them.

"We wait." He shrugged out of his vest and tossed it onto the sofa. "While we're waiting, you can tell me everything you know about David Jannisek. What you don't know, I'll fill in from the investigation we ran on him. He's got to believe you're Becky when he calls.''

''*If* he calls.''

''He will.''

''How can you be so sure?''

He flicked her a glance she couldn't interpret.

''Tell me,'' she insisted.

''Let me put it this way,'' he said with a grin, mimicking her words of a few minutes ago. ''If your sister looks half as good in that purple string thing we found in her living room as you did in a similar number last night, he'd be crazy *not* to call.''

To Lauren's consternation, a fiery heat started beneath her collarbones and pushed its way to her cheeks. She couldn't remember the last time she'd blushed. Junior high, maybe. Certainly not since Becky had clued her in on the facts of life.

Even more annoying, her skin prickled like mad.

This was, she thought grimly, going to be a long day.

It turned out to be even longer than she envisioned.

Marsh didn't waste time starting his interrogation. As soon as she'd shed the suede jacket, he emptied the contents of a thick file on the table.

Lauren's throat went dry at the sight of her sister's license photo, blown up to blurry proportions. Under it was another shot, this one in black and white. Her heart clutched as she lifted it.

Oversize sunglasses and a wide-brimmed straw hat all but obscured Becky's face as she laughed up at the man at her side, but her vitality leaped from the glossy print.

Oh, Beck, Lauren thought, you can't laugh your way out of it this time. Sighing, she shifted her gaze to her sister's escort.

"Is that David Jannisek?"

Marsh flicked a glance at the photograph in her hand. Lauren got the distinct impression that his disdain for Jannisek bordered on animosity. Maybe all cops felt that way about those walking the narrow path between legitimacy and the mob.

"That's him."

Becky certainly hadn't exaggerated when she'd described her latest love as tall, tanned, blond and too blasted handsome for his own good. He was all that and more. He should have looked four decades out of date in that pencil-thin mustache, silk ascot, and navy blazer, but somehow he managed to carry the absurd ensemble off with careless panache.

"What did your sister tell you about him?"

"Not much," she admitted. "Only that he's funny, he prefers dogs to cats, and he likes to live well."

"No kidding. Take a look at that report under your hand."

Shocked and more than a little staggered by what she read, Lauren skimmed a report that painted a vivid picture of Jannisek's extravagant life-style. Although he'd dug himself into a deep hole long before he met Becky, she'd put her hand on the spade, too. Lauren squirmed uncomfortably when she read the reports detailing the gifts the hotelier had purchased for her sister.

Evidently David Jannisek appreciated her sister's taste in lingerie as much as Marsh did. He'd footed the bill for three hundred dollars' worth at an exclusive Scottsdale boutique. He'd shelled out, too, for the new CD player recently installed in Becky's car, as well as a weekend fling at a resort in Palm Springs and cosmetic laser surgery to blast away the strawberry-shaped mole on her sister's right hip.

Then there was the diamond unicorn. It had to go back. It would go back, Lauren promised silently, as soon as she could arrange it.

"He also," Marsh informed her, dryly, "wagered almost twenty thousand dollars at the track the last time he took your sister there for an afternoon of sun and fun."

"She couldn't have known he was betting that much!"

"Maybe. Maybe not." His gaze drifted to her hair. "He put ten thousand on a three-year-old filly in the last race, by the way. Her name was Red," he drawled. "Red Delight, out of Dancer's Delight."

Lauren's cheeks heated again, this time on Becky's behalf. "Even if my sister knew David Jannisek was throwing money around like that, she must have thought he could cover his bets.''

''Then she thought wrong. What did she tell you about the guy?''

Lauren exhausted her meager store of information long before it satisfied her inquisitor. He spent the rest of the morning alternately grilling her and willing David Jannisek to call. By eleven, she had a headache that wouldn't quit. By noon, Marsh had taken to prowling the cabin like a caged lion.

Watching him, she itched for a pencil and her sketchbooks. The animal allegory wasn't all that far off. She'd position him against a natural backdrop, she decided. Facing a cougar, high atop a mountain ledge. Or a panther snarling out his dominance over his jungle territory. The hunter and the hunted.

The concept fit him, but didn't exactly make her feel any more comfortable with the situation. As much to keep busy as anything else, Lauren insisted on taking her turn in the kitchen preparing lunch.

After a meal of sandwiches and sliced tomatoes, the afternoon dragged endlessly. A quick call to Josh didn't help matters. The museum director was *not* happy about the canceled meeting, and, no, he hadn't finished the color screens for the Breckinridge note cards. Discouraged, Lauren left him Marsh's cellphone number.

Several times during the long afternoon, she thought about calling Becky. She wanted to make sure her sister had arrived safely at Aunt Jane's. She also wanted to talk to her about David Jannisek.

The reports she'd read earlier had shaken her. Hearing from Marsh that the handsome hotelier had involved her sister in his troubles with the mob was bad enough. Seeing it in print left Lauren with a sick feeling in the pit of her stomach. She hadn't realized Becky had become so involved with the man, or that they'd spent a vacation together in Palm Springs. Doubts plagued her more and more. With Marsh growing more tense with each hour the phone didn't ring, Lauren wondered again if she'd done the right thing by trying to shield her sister.

Her doubts came crashing up against hard reality a little after four o'clock. Edgy and taut, Marsh announced he was going to haul in some firewood. Stuffing a pair of canvas work gloves into his hip pocket, he grabbed the leather sling beside the fireplace.

Lauren snatched up her borrowed jacket and followed. She needed exercise and fresh air as much as a break from the mounting tension. She'd just stepped onto the porch when the unmistakable crack of rifle fire shattered the stillness.

Marsh spun in the direction of the shot.

Lauren screamed and threw herself off the porch steps in a clumsy swan dive. Her right shoulder hit Marsh in the back, taking him down a half second before another sharp crack split the air.

Chapter 8

The flying tackle hit Marsh square in the back. Survival skills pounded into him by four brawny brothers and his long years in the field had him twisting in mid-air to grapple with his attacker.

He landed on his back with a thud that rattled his bones. Lauren came down on top of him, all flying hair and sharp elbows. One of her knees gouged into his hip. The other came down on his thigh. He protected himself—barely—with another sharp twist to the side.

"What in the hell…?"

"Stay down!" Frantic, she dragged on his vest to keep him flat to the ground. "Didn't you hear those shots?"

"I heard them." He grabbed at her scrabbling hands. "Lauren, I heard them! It's okay."

"It's not okay!" She burrowed her face into his shoulder. "Someone's shooting at us!"

"Not at us. At the sky."

He wasn't sure she'd heard him. She remained planted facedown in his vest. Her body stretched taut and trembling atop his. Marsh felt the electric contact from his neck to his knees. A distant part of his mind noted how perfectly her hips fit against his. A not-so-distant part focused on the way her breasts flattened on his chest. Sternly repressing the response her squirming body roused in his, he shifted to one side.

"It's okay," he murmured again, calming her with the same soothing voice he'd use on a spooked mare. "That was one of the good guys. The bad guys wouldn't announce themselves."

Or miss two easy targets. Marsh kept that particular observation to himself as she dragged her head up a mere millimeter.

"What do you mean, 'announce themselves'?"

The utter confusion on her face had him biting back a smile. "How would I know to deactivate the perimeter alarms unless a visitor lets me know he's coming?"

"For Pete's sake, tell them to just *call* next time!"

Thoroughly indignant, she pushed up with both hands. The small movement separated their chests—and canted her hips into his.

With her body fitted so intimately against his, Marsh couldn't have told anyone a damned thing at that moment. As it was, he could barely move enough to dig a hand into his back pocket. A quick press deactivated the electronic sensors.

"What did you think you were doing, anyway?" he got out through gritted teeth, as she rolled off him.

"I didn't think," she admitted. Still shaken, she rose up on her knees and shoved her hair out of her eyes. "I heard the shot and just sort of...reacted."

Like last night, when she'd snatched a lid off a garbage can and prepared to do battle with a supposed housebreaker. Or when she'd come up out of a tangle of blankets after tumbling off the bunk, scared to death but ready to protect herself against an unseen foe.

Admiration rippled through Marsh, layering right on top of the heat she'd ignited in his belly. The woman had guts. A mouth made for kissing, a body right out of a man's most private fantasies, a fierce loyalty to her flaky sister, and guts. The combination left him sweating.

"Yeah, well, reacting is *my* job," he reminded her, pushing up on one elbow. "If someone *had* been shooting at us, you wouldn't have helped matters by landing on top of me and impeding my movements."

"Well, excuse me for trying to save your life."

"If anything comes down that doesn't sound or feel right, just take cover, okay, and let me handle the situation."

Her face set into stubborn lines, but before she

could argue, the crunch of iron-shod hooves sounded on the path behind them, followed a moment later by a raspy, smoke-roughened voice.

"That you, boy?"

Marsh bit back a groan. He'd recognize that froggy croak anywhere.

"Yeah, Shad, it's me."

"What the hell you doin' on your butt in the dirt?"

"Just admiring the view."

Rolling to his feet, he reached down a hand to help Lauren up. Over her head, he shot a warning look at the grizzled cowboy leaning on his saddle horn. The old man ignored it.

"I see what you mean, boy." A grin split his whisker-fuzzed cheeks. "She's a durned sight prettier than that hoity-toity, yellow-haired stockbroker you brought up here last time."

All too conscious of the stare Lauren turned on him, Marsh aimed another warning at their visitor. "This is business, Shad. DEA business."

The barb bounced right off the leathery hide of the man who'd hooted with laughter every time one of the Henderson boys had gone flying off a half-broke bronc, and then dusted them off and put them right back in the saddle.

"If you say so, boy." Unperturbed, he fired a stream of tobacco juice into the grass and swung off his horse. "You gonna introduce me to your DEA business, or just stand there like a wart on a hog?"

"Lauren Smith. Shadrach McCoy."

"Shadrach?" she echoed. "Like in Shadrach, Meshach and...?"

"Abednego," the old man finished, chuckling. "Pleased to meet a woman who knows her Old Testament, Ms. Smith."

To Marsh's astonishment, the foreman took the hand she extended and bowed over it with knob-kneed grace.

Lauren was utterly charmed. Her face lit up in a wide, warm smile. "Thank you, Mr. McCoy."

"Call me Shad, ma'am. Everyone does."

"Shad."

The syrupy exchange put a little burr under Marsh's skin. Shad was more than twice his age and three times as ornery, yet with a few short phrases he'd raised a smile from Lauren that could melt the snows on the peaks. She certainly hadn't turned one like that on Marsh.

"What brings you up here?" he asked the foreman.

The question came out sounding brusque, even to his own ears. One of Shad's shaggy gray brows shot up, and then arrowed down almost to the bridge of his nose.

"Just came up to make sure the boys had hauled in the supplies and fuel you asked for."

"They did. We're set."

"Y'are, huh?" His raisin-black eyes shifted. "What about you, ma'am? You need anything?"

Lauren could think of a hundred things she needed. An appointment with a shrink to have her head examined for driving off with a complete stranger headed the list. Comfortable underwear ran a close second. She couldn't ask Shadrach McCoy to supply either, however.

"No. Thank you, I'm fine."

"Y'are, huh?"

His bushy brows went to work again. Up, down, up. Whatever he saw in her face put a twinkle in his eye, but his expression was bland when he turned back to Marsh.

"Well, I'll let you get back to admirin' the view."

He reached for the reins. Leather creaked as he swung into the saddle.

"But you might want to move your admirin' inside, boy. Be a shame if a pocket gopher ran up your pant leg, like the one…"

"Shad…"

"…that scooted up your jeans when you were wrasslin' with your brothers," he continued amiably, ignoring the growled warning. "Chewed a good-sized bite outa your be-hind, as I recall."

With a tip of his hat, he kneed his mount around.

Lauren took one look at Marsh's face and swallowed a giggle. Red singed his cheeks. Evidently losing a chunk of his be-hind to a gopher didn't square with his tough guy image.

"Have you known him long?"

"Shad?" He followed the grizzled veteran's progress through the pines with a combination of wry

resignation and undisguised affection. "All my life.
I grew up around these parts."

So he was a native of this rugged country. That
explained the black Stetson and his familiarity with
an iron skillet. It didn't, however, explain the hoity-
toity stockbroker.

Was she the one who'd burned him? The one
whose memory raised that bleak look in his eyes
when Lauren joked about finding a paragon of trust
and hanging on to her with both hands? She couldn't
imagine Marsh Henderson letting go of a woman
without a fight. Couldn't imagine any woman wanting him to.

The thought shocked her. So did the inescapable
fact that the man now fascinated her almost as much
as his grim determination to track down a mob boss
unnerved her. She'd never been attracted to tough,
muscled cowboy-cop types before. Her former husband was an ad exec. The few men she'd dated since
her divorce shared her passion for visual, not mar-
tial, arts.

Yet Lauren had the sinking feeling that the more
she learned about the man behind the blue and gold
shield, the more she'd want to know. Like what had
happened to the stockbroker. And just where the gopher had done his dastardly deed.

With that impossible, irrepressible thought swirl-
ing around in her head, she accompanied Marsh
while he resumed his interrupted task of hauling in
firewood. Someone—no doubt the ranch hands Shad
had mentioned—had cut, split, and stacked several

cords of wood between two tall pines at the back of the cabin. When Marsh spread the two-handled sling beside the stack, Lauren moved to help him.

"I'll do it," he told her, reaching into his back pocket. "You need gloves to handle this stuff."

While he tugged on the canvas work gloves, she fingered an orangy furrow in the dark-colored bark. "What is it?"

"Ponderosa pine. Some call it yellow pine."

He tossed two hefty logs on the sling, swung back for two more with a natural rhythm that said he'd performed this task before. Lauren found herself intrigued by the smooth coordination of man and muscle.

"The Anasazi who used to live in these parts used the bark to make small, hot cook fires," he added conversationally. "The fires gave off no smoke and cooled rapidly, so they could disperse the ashes and leave no trace of their presence."

"Unlike modern man, who leaves his mark everywhere. I saw the stands of new growth this morning where loggers have harvested the forest."

"Most of the ranchers around here derive a good part of their income from timber leases," he said with a shrug that made no apologies to environmentalists. "The federal and state forestry folks control the harvesting, but the ponderosa is in high demand for its clear wood for frames, moldings and cabinetry."

"It smells like…" She scratched a nail along the bark, trying to identify the elusive scent.

"Vanilla," he supplied with a grin. "On hot days, you could walk through these woods and swear you were in an ice-cream shop."

He was right. Even now, with the fall nipping at the air, a sweet aroma mingled with the earthy mix of bark and pine.

"I used to suck on the stuff as a kid." He transferred more logs to the sling, and then broke off a little twig sprouting from a knothole. "Here, take a lick."

She shook her head in smiling refusal. "No, thanks. Wood isn't on my diet."

"You don't know what you're missing."

"I don't *want* to know what I'm missing. I bet there are worms crawling around in that."

"Coward."

Long afterward, Lauren would blame the idiocy that came next on the laughter glinting in his blue eyes. And the trickle of sweat that traced a silver streak from just under his jaw down his neck. And his nearness, which shrank to minuscule proportions when he propped a boot on a log and tempted her with the same teasing persuasion Eve must have used on Adam.

"I'll take the first taste. Then you try it."

"Oh, yech! You're not really going to lick that, are you?"

He was, and he did. After a serious swipe, he smacked his lips. "Mmm, delicious."

"I'll take your word for it," she said on a hiccup of laughter.

"You don't have to." He leaned forward another inch or two. "Here, you can taste it on me."

He made the offer with such casual nonchalance that Lauren hesitated only for a second or two before tipping her head toward his. She'd only take a taste—just brush her lips against his.

The problem became apparent the moment her mouth met his. One taste wasn't enough. For either of them. She drew back, startled by the electricity generated by the brief contact. From the sudden, slashing frown on Marsh's face, he had experienced the same power burst she did.

He muttered something, some indistinct reference to a plan. Then his arm slid around her waist, his head bent, and his mouth came down on hers.

Lauren had never believed Becky's nonsense about bells clanging and whistles sounding and rockets going off every time she fell in love. Lauren herself had certainly never heard much more than a tinkle or two, even during those first, heady months of her courtship and marriage.

Marsh's kiss came darned close to making a believer out of her. Her ears buzzed, not from whistles or bells or rockets, but from the little bursts of pleasure that exploded inside her.

This was crazy. She'd met the man less than twenty-four hours ago. She still didn't quite trust him. Yet she arched into him, cursing the layers of suede and flannel and denim that separated them. Within seconds, pleasure spiraled into greed. Within moments, greed galloped into hunger.

A lifetime later, one of them—she couldn't say who—ended the shattering kiss. Her heart hammering under her borrowed jacket, Lauren was the first to break the taut silence.

"You're..." She swallowed, and then swiped her tongue along her lower lip. "...you're right. It does taste like vanilla."

With a silent curse, Marsh dragged his gaze from her glistening lips. Dammit, making love to the woman was *not* part of his plan! It would only complicate matters, not to mention take the edge off his concentration. Hell, he'd hardly slept last night as it was.

He couldn't believe he'd given in to the insane impulse to drag her up against him and kiss her like that. He'd intended to make it light, keep the game going between them, put her at ease with that silliness about the tree bark. Instead, he'd come within half a heartbeat of backing her against the woodpile, unpeeling that jacket, and taking up where his fantasies had left off last night. No wonder her brown eyes now regarded him with that combination of confusion and wariness.

He felt every bit as wary, but not confused. The tight, hot spark Lauren ignited in him left no room for confusion. He wanted her. The want had been building in him all day. Correction, all day and what had been left of last night after he'd charged into the bunk room and found her tangled up in blankets, half a T-shirt and a couple of strings.

He'd kept himself under control, though, until she

took her swan dive off the porch and landed on top of him. Marsh had felt her on every square inch of his body. Could *still* feel her. He had to pull rein, and fast.

Mustering as much nonchalance as he could given the fact that he ached in ways he hadn't ached in longer than he could remember, he summoned a grin.

"Just don't confuse the ponderosa with the Douglas fir. They're both long and tall and red-barked, but the Douglas resin could take the enamel off your teeth."

She nodded, her eyes still wary. "I'll remember that the next time someone offers me a bite of tree."

Her guarded expression said she wasn't any happier about what had just happened than he was. Good! He wanted her to keep up her guard, just as he intended to.

Convinced he'd put matters back on the right track with his show of nonchalance, Marsh stripped off the gloves and stuffed them in his back pocket.

"How do steaks grilled over an open flame sound for supper?"

"Good," she replied, easing into the same neutral tone, "as long as you do the grilling. I've never cooked over open flames before."

"Nothing to it." Gathering the handles of the carrier in one fist, he hefted the heavy load. "The trick is to let them sear, but not burn."

That was the trick all right, Lauren thought, as she watched Marsh at work before the stone fireplace an hour later. The leaping flames burnished his skin to a tawny gold. His black hair gleamed wet at the temples from his quick wash-up. Fat dripping from the steaks pressed into a long-handled grill sizzled and spit in the flames, providing the only sound in the room.

Lauren tucked her feet under her on the sofa, frowning at the back of Marsh's head. She wasn't stupid. The message he'd sent after that mind-blowing kiss had come through loud and clear. He'd enjoyed it as much as she had, but he'd brought her up here on business. She'd darned well better not forget it was deadly business, one that demanded his full concentration. He might lighten up a little and let a smile slip out on occasion, but he wasn't going to let anything distract him from his primary mission.

Fine. Lauren didn't want to distract him. Not really.

Or at least…not much.

She squirmed on the lumpy sofa cushions, not particularly happy with the realization that she'd pulled a Becky this afternoon. She'd tumbled into Marsh's arms without stopping to think of the consequences—like the fact that their enforced proximity would take one kiss and magnify it a hundred times in her head. She *had* to stop thinking about it!

Scowling, she pulled her gaze from his broad back and to the plates, utensils and cold beers that sat on the scrubbed pine coffee table in front of her, along with a small black-bottomed pan centered on a thick potholder. Lauren's sole contribution to the evening meal had been to open and heat up a can of pork and beans. Nothing to divert her thoughts there.

"What did you mean by a plan?" she asked, as much to break the silence as anything else.

He swiveled around on one heel. The steaks he'd been turning over the flames took a dip.

"What?"

"A while ago, right before we…kissed." She willed herself not to break into another schoolgirl blush, the way she had earlier this morning. "I thought you muttered something about a plan."

"You must have misunderstood me."

"No, I'm…" Her eyes widened as flames engulfed the steaks and danced along the grill handle where the grease had run. "Marsh! Look out!"

He jerked around, cursing. A moment later, two charred rib eyes hit the plate. The chagrin on his face had Lauren biting back a smile.

"I like mine well done."

"Good thing," he replied wryly.

The tension between them eased. Not completely, but enough for Lauren to enjoy both her meal and the bits Marsh let drop about growing up in this part of the country. He had four brothers, she learned, and from the irreverent tales he told about their rough-and-tumble childhood, it was obvious he felt as close a tie to them as she felt toward Becky.

They washed their few dishes and Lauren called

it a day not long after. Night had dropped like a stone, shrouding the cabin in darkness. Not until she'd crawled under the blankets did she remember the conversation interrupted by the burning steaks. With a shrug, she dismissed Marsh's odd reluctance to talk about this plan of his. She was probably better off not knowing, she thought wryly. The less the bait knew about the hunter's intentions, the more soundly she'd sleep.

Besides, she was starting to believe David Jannisek wasn't going to try to find Becky. Twenty-four hours had passed since he had called the Valley of the Sun Inn. After another twenty-four hours, forty-eight at most, even Marsh would have to admit that they couldn't stay holed up here indefinitely.

The next evening proved her wrong on both counts. David Jannisek called Special Agent Pepper Dennis at the DEA from a pay phone just over the border between Nevada and California, wanting to know how he could reach Becky.

Agent Dennis in turn called Marsh, who proceeded to inform Lauren that they were going to sit right where they were until her sister's boyfriend contacted her.

Chapter 9

Lauren paced back and forth before the stone fireplace. The early-evening twilight slanting through the cabin windows painted her in vivid colors.

"What did he say? Exactly."

Ankles crossed on the sturdy coffee table, Marsh followed her agitated pacing like a spectator at a tennis match. He didn't have to think about his answer. David Jannisek's short conversation with Pepper Dennis, relayed to him just a half hour ago, had burned into his brain.

"One, he'd heard Becky was in the custody of a DEA agent. Two, he wanted to know why. Three, he wanted to know where."

"He didn't ask if she was okay? If she was scared or worried or anything?"

"I expect he'll ask those questions when he decides to call you."

She shot a disgruntled glance at the cellphone resting beside Marsh's boot on the coffee table. "He's taking his time about it."

"You might take some time, too, if you had to choose between the cops or the mob."

The mild comment earned him an evil look. Marsh took it in stride. The wait was beginning to wear on Lauren's nerves. She'd been restless all day and had bristled like a caged cat ever since Pepper's call.

Marsh's nerves, on the other hand, had settled into the icy calm he felt just before a take-down. His long years of hunting both four-legged and two-legged prey had taught him not to rush things at this crucial point. The target was sniffing at the bait. All Marsh had to do now was wait—quietly, patiently—until the quarry stepped into his gun sights.

He also, he reflected wryly as Lauren took another agitated turn, had to make sure his bait didn't come apart at the seams.

"We could be talking anywhere from a few more hours to a few more days yet. If I were Jannisek, I'd be thinking hard about my options right now."

"A few more days!" she echoed, dismay written all over her expressive face.

"My gut tells me it won't take that long. Relax, Lauren."

"Ha! That's easy for you to say. Your sister isn't

the one who got herself all tangled up with a man with ties to the mob.''

Marsh's jaw tightened. Maybe it was time to tell her about Ellen's brutal murder. He started to tell her. He *wanted* to tell her. He might have forced out the words if she hadn't rounded on him at that moment.

''I've got to talk to Becky.'' She scooped up the cellphone, her brown eyes challenging his across the coffee table. ''Will you try to trace this call?''

He dropped his gaze and contemplated the toe of his boot. He could lie to her. It certainly wouldn't be the first time. He'd lied by inference if not in actual fact when he'd staged that break-in at her sister's house. He was still lying by not disclosing that his hunt for the man who tried to take out Jannisek wasn't official, but all-too personal.

The lies didn't come as easily after two days in her company, however. He lifted his gaze to hers and gave her what assurances he could.

''I promised you I wouldn't let anything happen to you or your sister. That's all I'll promise.''

Obviously torn, she hesitated for several moments, then whirled and stalked into the bunk room. The door slammed behind her.

Feeling ridiculously hurt by his refusal to give even an inch, Lauren dropped down on her bunk. Why couldn't Marsh grant her immunity for one blasted phone call? She'd gone along with his schemes, offered herself up in Becky's stead, and agreed to this incarceration halfway up a mountain.

Yet he refused to respect her need to protect her sister as best she could.

She wanted to talk to Becky, wanted to make sure she'd received the money Josh had wired and arrived at Aunt Jane's safely. Even more important, she wanted to warn her sister that David Jannisek was searching for her. Chewing on the inside of her cheek, Lauren thought for a moment, then punched in her office number.

"Artworks, Incorporated."

"Josh, this is me.

"I hope you're calling me from thirty thousand feet, on your way back to Denver."

"No. It may be a few more days yet."

"You gotta be kidding!"

Lauren only wished she was.

"I need you here," he protested. "These color screens are giving me fits. And you've got the monthly breakfast meeting of the Women Entrepreneurs of Denver tomorrow, remember?"

She brushed aside the color screens and the valuable networking meeting. She couldn't think about business right now.

"Cancel the breakfast meeting. Get my Aunt Jane on the other line for me, will you? Her number's in the Rolodex on my desk."

She waited with toe-tapping impatience for Josh to make the connection.

"Okay, she's on."

"Say hi for me, and tell her I need to speak to Becky."

Josh put her on hold and was back a moment later. "She says hi, and Becky's not there. She took off."

Lauren's knuckles went white on the phone. "What do you mean, she took off?"

The rejected suitor couldn't resist putting in his two cents worth. "My guess is that she's gone for a joyride with the local Harley salesman."

"Just ask Jane!"

"What did I tell you?" he replied after a pause that seemed to stretch forever. "Becky pulled her usual stunts. She stayed one night with your aunt, cleaned her out of ready cash and faded into the sunset."

"Where'd she go?"

The long-suffering intermediary relayed the question and subsequent answer. "Your aunt doesn't know where. All Becky said was that she had to see a man about a ring."

"A ring? What ring?"

"The one she put through the poor fool's nose, probably."

Feeling shell-shocked, Lauren flipped the phone shut a few moments later and stared helplessly at Miss January. She couldn't believe Becky had just taken off like that. Her sister generally acted when the impulse struck her, but surely she'd have more sense than to disappear after Lauren's urgent warnings.

As the numbness began to wear off, a thousand horrible possibilities started chasing through her mind. Maybe Becky had been followed to Aunt Jane's. Maybe she'd spotted someone watching her. Maybe she was trying to draw them away from Aunt Jane and was running for her life.

Oh, God!

Calling herself a hundred kinds of an idiot, Lauren surged to her feet. She shouldn't have tried to play this dangerous game herself. She should have told Marsh exactly where Becky was and let him take her into protective custody.

Her insides shaking, she yanked open the door.

One look at her face brought Marsh off the sofa. "What's the problem?"

"Becky's..." She returned the phone to the coffee table, fighting tears. "Becky's..."

Panic for her sister and the horrible feeling that she'd messed up big time by not trusting the police to take care of Becky choked her.

"She's what?" His arms came around her. "Lauren, sweetheart! Tell me. Is she hurt?"

She sensed rather than heard the foreboding behind the question. His cop's mind was already working overtime, no doubt envisioning even more grim possibilities than Lauren had.

She sniffed into his shirtfront and blurted out the truth. "She's gone."

"Gone where?"

"I don't know! She just...took off."

She had to let go of his shirt. Had to face him. Had to face, too, the consequences of her misguided attempts to protect her sister.

She would. She'd take a deep breath, release her death grip and pour out the whole story. In a minute or two. As soon as she could bring herself to break the circle of his arms.

Marsh didn't let her break anything. Keeping her cradled against his chest, he waited for her to work through her choking panic. When she calmed enough, he eased them both down. She was still clinging to his now-damp shirtfront when he settled them both on the sofa.

To her surprise, he didn't grill her for details right away. He held her, just held her. He'd laid a fire while she was in the other room, she saw from the corner of one eye. Flames danced above the orange-barked logs. A faint vanilla scent drifted above the tang of burning wood. Only after she'd drawn in several long, shudder-free breaths did his low request rumble in her ear.

"Tell me what happened."

Sighing, Lauren lifted her head. She told him everything. Her suggestion that her sister hide out at Aunt Jane's. Her belief Becky would be safe there. Her three-way call with Josh. Marsh listened without interruption, processing the information as she related it.

"I told her to stay in Albuquerque," she finished miserably. "Aunt Jane isn't really a blood relation, just a longtime family friend. No one would have known to look for my sister at her house."

"Then it's a safe bet no one did."

Panic fluttered in her chest again. "How do you

know? The mob has all kinds of connections. All kinds of resources. Maybe they followed her, or put some kind of electronic tracking device on her car, or..."

"Trust me. If I couldn't find Becky, they couldn't either."

"But you stopped looking for her when you found me!"

A black brow cocked. "You think so?"

Lauren was shocked to realize he'd been working against her for the past two days, and just relieved enough to let it go. Desperate for reassurance, she clutched at the straw he offered.

"So you don't think anyone followed her to my aunt's?"

"My guess is they didn't."

The quiet reply went a long way to soothing Lauren's panicky guilt. His breath fanning warm and steady against her temple went even further.

Only after she pulled away a little did she realize that his calm was for her benefit. Up close and personal like this, she could see the tension in his jaw as he stared over her head into the fire.

"What does this do to your scheme to trap David Jannisek?"

Those incredible blue eyes shifted. He looked at her—through her—for a long moment.

How *did* Becky Smith's second disappearance affect his plan? His mind racing, Marsh sorted through the possible ramifications. When Becky had slipped through his fingers, he'd played the odds that Jannisek didn't know where she was. Did he dare play those odds a second time?

Would Lauren go along with him if he did?

He focused on the face turned up to his. Tears had clumped her dark lashes and left damp traces on her cheeks. Her mouth, that warm, generous, sexy mouth he'd tasted yesterday and dreamed about most of the night, had thinned with worry.

When he thought of all he'd put her through, all she'd gone through to protect her sister, something wrenched inside him. Deeper than worry, sharper than guilt, it cracked the hard shell he'd encased himself in since Ellen's death. Just a little. Just enough for him to lift a hand and brush a damp strand of hair from her cheek.

"I'm not changing strategies," he told her, quietly. "I've got to play the odds that Jannisek still thinks I have Becky. To lessen those odds, though, I'll have my partner beef up the trace on her car. Now that I know where she was yesterday, maybe we can track her down."

She nodded numbly. Digging her hands in her pockets, she hunched her shoulders and waited while he passed Becky's last known location to Pepper.

"Get the New Mexico state police on it," he instructed. "We don't know where she went from Albuquerque, but someone must have spotted her."

He hung up a moment later and turned to Lauren. Her wobbly smile cut at his heart.

"I'm sorry I didn't trust you back at Becky's house. She might be in safe custody now."

"Lauren..."

"I'm trusting you now, Marsh. I'll help you however I can."

Dammit, didn't she realize that she shouldn't trust anyone in a situation like this, particularly a man torn between the need to maintain a necessary distance and the aching desire to lay her back on the sofa and kiss away the tear streaks?

"You don't need to scowl at me like that," she told him, her smile still shaky. "I'll bring Jannisek in for you. I can do a pretty convincing Becky if I put my mind to it."

When he didn't reply, she dropped her lashes. A moment later, they lifted once more. The kittenish pout on her mouth had him sucking in a sharp breath.

"What do you think?" she whispered in a throaty purr.

Her hand lifted to curl on his neck. Her fingers played with his nape. The hair on the back of Marsh's neck shot needles of fire straight into his skin.

"I think," he got out in a low growl, "that Becky probably took lessons in driving men crazy from her baby sister."

"You do?" Surprise and delight lit her face. "No kidding?"

He couldn't help it. He had to kiss her. Just once.

"No kidding."

He intended it to end right there. Even with her taste blazing on his lips, he was ready to unwrap his arms, push off the sofa and take a long walk in the chilly dusk that was now blanketing the windows. And he would have done exactly that if her delight hadn't melted into a self-deprecating shake of her head.

"My ex used to say all the time that he wished I'd take a few pages from Becky's book and spice up our life."

"Your ex is an ass."

He said it with such absolute authority that she grinned, and he had to kiss her again. Since her arm was still curled around his neck, it was a simple matter of logistics to ease her back against the sofa cushions and indulge in a long, thorough mating of lips to lips and thighs to thighs.

His knee found a spot between hers. One hand slid around her waist to trace the bumpy ridge of her spine. The other got lost in her hair. Anchored in the windblown tangle, it tipped her head back and Marsh wasted no time deepening the kiss.

The sensation was indescribable, like plunging down a steep, wooded slope on a half-broke mustang. Marsh felt his heart jump straight into his throat. Felt, too, the wild exhilaration of the ride. It seemed to take forever, and ended far too soon for his satisfaction. His breath rasped hard and fast when he pulled back. A fierce satisfaction shot through him when he saw his exploding hunger reflected in her eyes.

"This is crazy," he growled, dipping down to lick her lower lip. She was addictive, like tangy barbecue sauce on sizzling ribs or cold watermelon on a hot day. He couldn't get enough of her.

"Crazy," she echoed, her mouth as hungry as his.

"We should stop now, before it's too late."

"You first," she panted.

Even before his tongue found hers, Marsh knew he was making a mistake. Come morning, he'd regret mixing his deadly business with this wicked pleasure. Come morning, his nagging guilt for using her like this would have eaten even deeper into his gut.

But tonight...

Tonight, dammit, he wanted her. No, he craved her with a sudden, driving urgency that shoved every rational consideration from his mind, leaving only a kaleidoscope of irrational and erotic thoughts, not the least of which was a burning desire to unsnap her jeans, slide them down her hips, and treat himself to another glimpse of her lacy little thong.

Just the memory of her trim flanks and rounded bottom was enough to set his brain on fire, not to mention all parts south. He'd work his way down to the thong, he promised himself. Slowly. Piece by piece. Enjoying all the side trips and detours along the way.

His misplaced idea that he could take things at a measured pace went up in smoke the moment he slid his hand under the hem of her sweatshirt. Her belly hollowed under his palm, and her breath caught at the whisper of cool air on her rib cage.

"It's okay," he murmured, doubling down to drop a kiss on her tummy. "I'll warm you up."

She gave a choke of laughter at the smug promise, but it didn't take long for her skin to flame under his mouth and tongue and teeth.

It took exactly the same amount of time for Marsh to realize he had to get her out of her clothes, fast. Luckily, she had reached the same conclusion. In a flurry of arms and legs and bumping heads, they shed boots, sneakers, shirt and sweatshirt.

Marsh experienced a momentary setback when he caught sight of the plain, no-nonsense cotton bra she wore under the sweatshirt. To his relief, a teasing strip of lacy elastic peeked above the waistband of her jeans and gave him hope for what lay beneath. He managed a credible one-handed job on the snap and zipper, but when he peeled them down, her whole body went still.

Unfortunately, his didn't. He ached from his neck down, tight with wanting, hard with need. It took everything he had to drag his mouth from hers and lift his head.

"I can't..." She swiped her tongue along her swollen lips. "That is, I don't..."

"Don't what, sweetheart?"

"We'd better stop. I, uh, don't..."

She looked away, her face tinted pink.

His groin twisted. Okay. He got the message. She was trying to tell him she didn't want to take this any further. Marsh could accept that. He didn't like it, but he could accept it. Now all he had to do was rein in his raging need and...

"I don't have any protection."

Her indistinct mumble shot relief straight into his veins. Grinning, he catapulted to his feet.

"I do."

He'd scooped her up in his arms and headed for the bunk room.

"Oh. Right," she said coolly. "How could I forgot the hoity-toity stockbroker?"

He kicked open the door, unperturbed by the tiny crease that settled between her brows.

"This is a line shack, remember? Inhabited by a steady stream of horny ranch hands, seasonal hunters and the occasional female visitor. Unless I'm mistaken, there's a store of essential supplies on the shelf that could tide us over until spring."

The crease disappeared as Lauren looped her arms around his neck. "Just so there's enough to get us through tonight."

And tomorrow, Marsh thought, with a surge of need so fierce it stunned him. If Jannisek didn't call, they'd have tonight *and* tomorrow *and* maybe another night or two.

Disconcerted to find himself hoping that the quarry he'd hunted for so long didn't sniff at the bait for a few more days, he carried his half-naked burden across the bunk room. Propping her on one knee, he searched the dusty shelf for the boxes he and his brothers had stashed there over the years.

Voluptuous Miss January, the object of so many of his adolescent fantasies, smiled archly down at him. Marsh didn't spare her a glance. The woman in his arms fired his blood more than the calendar girl ever had.

He finally found what he was looking for on the dusty shelf. A moment later, he took Lauren and himself down on her bunk in a tumble of hot hands, tangled legs and greedy mouths.

Chapter 10

This was insane.

The refrain clamored in Lauren's head as she arched under Marsh. Breath ragged, her flesh flaming from the fire he stoked in her, she couldn't help but note the absurdities.

The bunk was too narrow. Their combined weight stretched the springs to their limit. Marsh was half on the bed, half hanging over the edge. Their knees knocked with every twist and turn. The scratchy blanket pricked her backside.

This was insane and *so* Becky!

It was also incredible.

Lauren had never lost herself so swiftly, had never wanted so hungrily. She couldn't remember the last time the scrape of a man's stubble against her collarbone had given her such delight. Or such exquisite torment.

Marsh used his hands and oh-so-clever mouth on her, playing her the way a virtuoso would a Steinway. Every nerve hummed. Every vein sang. The calluses on his palms raised tiny shivers as he stroked her from breast to hip, back to bottom. The dark, wiry hair on his legs and chest provided just enough abrasion to raise even more shivers.

Caught up in a spiral of rippling sensation, Lauren was just as eager to explore. One hand raked through his hair. The other sizzled with the tactile sensations of hard ridges, coiled muscle and heated flesh.

Her mouth was swollen from his kisses when he shifted his attention to her breasts. With a contortion that threatened to dump him over the side of the narrow bunk, he bent down. Lauren gasped when his tongue went to work on her rigid nipples, and groaned when he substituted teeth for tongue. But it wasn't until his fingers slid down her belly and hooked on the borrowed thong that her heart flip-flopped inside her chest.

"I've been in a serious sweat since I saw you in this little number the other night," he murmured against her quivering tummy.

That candid admission was enough to dampen the little number under discussion. Then he lifted his head, and damp gushed into wet. The grin he gave her was pure sex.

"Much as I enjoyed seeing you in it, I have to

confess I spent most of the day imagining you out of it.''

Looking up into his laughing eyes, Lauren vowed to hit the lingerie stores the moment she returned to civilization. To heck with comfort! So what if she walked funny for the rest of her life. If a tiny scrap of nylon and lace caused this kind of reaction in Marsh, she'd invest in an entire new wardrobe.

It wasn't until he'd begun to hook the panties down, inch by tantalizing inch, that reality pierced Lauren's spinning fantasies. A new wardrobe wouldn't cause any kind of reaction in Marsh, for the simple reason that there was no reason to believe he'd see it. They were together for tonight. Maybe tomorrow. Possibly the day after that. The realization sharpened her hunger to a near ache.

''You've got the sexiest knees,'' he announced as the thong made its slow descent. ''And ankles. I never thought of myself as an ankle man, but...'' He lifted first one foot, then her other. The panties disappeared. ''...you could make a believer out of me.''

She was wet and near to weeping with pleasure when he stretched out beside her. Her hands roamed his back, swept down to curve his waist. Marveling at the silky steel of his buns, she was searching surreptitiously for the exact location of the gopher bite when she noticed the hot-cold feel of his flesh. The chill mountain air was nipping at Marsh's rear with the same determination he was nipping at her lobe.

''Marsh, you're cold.''

"Not hardly."

Hunching a shoulder against the warm breath washing her ear, she groped under her for the scratchy wool blanket.

"Here..."

Grunting with the effort, she lifted her hips and tugged. Enough of the blanket came free to flip up and over them both. The effect was electric, like encasing hot coals in Reynolds Wrap. The wool trapped the heat between them and magnified it a hundred times. Lauren's skin went from warm and slick to fiery. The blackness surrounding them sizzled. Every pant sounded like thunder in her ears. Every twist and turn of their bodies generated more heat. When she was sure she would spontaneously combust, Marsh poured even more lighter fluid on the fires.

His mouth hard and hungry on hers, he cradled her with one arm, nudged her legs apart with a knee, and slid his hand through the tight curls of her mound. His fingers were gentle at first. Slow and deep and gentle. Then his thumb found her center, and the twin sensations of penetration and pressure nearly blew her away.

He was a magician, Lauren thought, in a gasp of wild pleasure. Marsh the magician. He knew just where to touch, just *how* to touch. She barely had time to wonder if he'd practiced these same sorcerer's skills on the hoity-toity stockbroker before he settled himself between her thighs.

His first thrust picked up the rhythm his hands

had already established. His second drove the sagging bedsprings almost to the floor. To Lauren's utter astonishment, she climaxed on the third.

She clenched her legs against the blinding rush of sensation. Tried desperately to hold it back. The waves came at her, harder, faster.

"Marsh! I can't...I don't...Ooooh!"

A thousand years later, she spun back to earth. A dark, scratchy, unfamiliar earth. Another thousand years passed before she realized he hadn't come apart at the seams with her.

He still filled her. Hard and hot and heavy. And still grinned down at her with a male smugness she couldn't miss even with a flap of blanket draped over his head.

"You," he pronounced, "are incredible."

Lauren fought her way through layer upon layer of sensual lassitude. Limp, she looped her arms around his neck. Languorous, she lifted both legs and wrapped them around his hips.

"So are you—when you're not playing big, bad cop and scaring me half to death."

This time it was Marsh who stiffened. Marsh whose muscles locked. Feeling more than a little smug herself at his reaction, Lauren summoned what was left of her strength and served him the same mind-shattering pleasure he'd served her.

She drifted out of her state of boneless satisfaction some time before he did his. For long moments, she lay still. Not that she could do anything else. Even with most of his weight balanced on his forearms, he took her and the mattress as far as the springs would go.

Darkness still shrouded them. The blanket had twisted around Marsh's legs, but covered his backside, back and head. Lauren was sure his contours had imprinted on hers. She was sure, too, that it would take her hours to regain her strength.

She was right on the first count, dead wrong on the second. Her breasts tingled from the rasp of his chest hair even after he roused enough to push up on his elbows. Yet when he maneuvered onto his side and brought her up against him, her back to his front, every nerve in her body started a slow dance. She cuddled against him, marveling at the sensation, until he broke the silence long moments later.

"Lauren."

"Mmm?"

"About this big, bad cop business."

"Mmm?"

He hesitated, his arms tight around her. "It's who I am."

The odd note in his voice worked its way through her sensual haze. He sounded almost apologetic, and very much as though he was issuing a warning. As if she needed a warning.

"We've established that you're a cop." A smile tugged at her mouth. "And you've certainly given new meaning to my definition of 'big'."

"Is that right?"

She couldn't mistake the inflection in his voice

this time. It was preening. Definitely preening. Her smile widened.

"And as for bad…"

She nudged backward, trying to find another inch or two on the crowded bunk. Her bottom made direct contact with what, until that moment, had been lazy, relaxed flesh.

"Bad, Mr. Henderson, is in the eye of the beholder."

His arm flexed, banding her against him. He held her still for a moment, as if fighting the urge that swept them both. Lauren held her breath until he bent over.

"I hope you remember that come morning, Ms. Smith."

With his whisper hot and husky in her ear and his body hard against hers, she doubted she'd remember anything come morning. After he brought her to a wild, panting climax for a second time, she could barely remember where she was at that particular moment.

Her last, confused thought before she sank into total oblivion was a vague prayer that Becky was safe and David Jannisek would take his time before contacting Marsh.

She woke the next morning to searing sunlight and the realization that she'd spent the entire night in the narrow bunk fitted like a spoon against Marsh. Her back to his chest, his knees tucked into hers, they occupied every square inch of bed space.

Bemused and more than a little stunned by her own reckless abandon, Lauren blinked the sleep from her eyes. The next bunk came into focus. The dust motes drifting on the slanting sunbeams. The potbellied stove. Finally, Miss January.

The pinup's smirk was even more pronounced this morning. With a sinking feeling, Lauren realized the overblown blonde had probably observed this same scene a dozen times. Maybe two dozen. As Marsh had pointed out, the line shack provided a handy refuge for horny ranch hands, seasonal hunters and DEA special agents.

Particularly DEA agents.

She shrugged aside a little pinprick of jealousy. It was too soon for jealousy and too late for regrets. More to the point, the hours she'd just spent in Marsh's arms most definitely fell into the unregrettable category. But that didn't lessen her morning-after mix of shyness, satisfaction and confusion. Drawing in a deep breath, she rolled over to find him raised up on one elbow, watching her.

His blue eyes were sleepy behind those ridiculously thick black lashes. Dark stubble shadowed his cheeks and chin. His skin stretched tan and smooth over bulging muscles and...

Lauren gasped, her gaze caught by the fist-sized scar almost covered by a swirl of dark chest hair. With one finger, she traced the circle of puckered skin.

"How did you get this?"

"A bullet went in and didn't want to come out."

She couldn't imagine any more sobering reminder of their teasing give-and-take about cops last night. No wonder he'd issued that warning.

With a gulp, she remembered that he hadn't brought her up here to play games—as fun as they were. He was here on business. A deadly business that could eventually lead to a man who'd already tried to kill at least once. The thought put a lump in her throat.

Swallowing, she leaned over and kissed the scarred tissue. Muscle and skin jumped under her lips. Marsh's hand burrowed into her hair. With a tug that was more surprising than painful, he pulled her head back.

"Lauren..."

"What?"

When he didn't answer, she put her own spin on his silence. Oh, God! Maybe the bullet was still in there. Maybe those groans she'd dragged out of him last night sprang from pain, not pleasure. An agony of remorse swept through her.

"Does it still hurt? You should have told me! We could have..." She flopped a hand helplessly. "...taken things a little easier."

Marsh stared down at her stricken face, and could swear he heard another crack in the hard shell he'd constructed around himself. His reaction to that featherlight kiss had been pure instinct, a gut-deep need to spare her the ugliness of the wound that had driven away the woman he'd once loved.

Except Lauren didn't seem to mind the ugliness.

And, he acknowledged in wry response to her question, it didn't hurt anymore. It hadn't hurt in a long time. In fact, he was damned if he could even remember his fiancée's face with Lauren's filling his vision.

"No, it doesn't hurt," he told her on a low laugh. "And no, we couldn't have taken things easier. Any easier and I would have died before you…"

A distant sound cut off his teasing reply. Marsh's head whipped up. The fist still buried in Lauren's hair tightened. He didn't realize how much until his glance cut swiftly back to her.

She hadn't made a sound. Not a whimper. But her jaw was clenched against the pull on her scalp.

"Damn!" He loosened his grip, his own jaw tight. "I'm sorry."

She brushed aside his apology. "What did you hear?"

"A car. Or truck. I'm not sure. We'd better get dressed."

Marsh snatched up the weapon he'd placed within easy reach beside the bunk and raced for the other room to retrieve his clothes. Lauren dug frantically in her bag for something to cover her nakedness. Marsh was dressed and checking his weapon when she rushed out of the bunk room, wearing a skimpy T-shirt and not much else. Snatching up her baggy sweatshirt, she dragged it on.

The Glock slid into its leather nest and settled with a familiar weight at the small of his back.

"Stay here until I give you the all clear. Lauren! Do you hear me?"

Her head poked through the sweatshirt. "I'm in this, too, Marsh."

"I know you are. It's probably Shad, or one of the other hands from the Bar-H coming up to check on us. Just give me time to check it out, okay?" He raked a hand through his hair to flatten it and pinned on a hopeful smile. "Some coffee would be nice, too."

"Okay, okay," she muttered, grabbing her jeans.

Marsh took the gut-clenching sight of her wiggling into her jeans with him. It hovered in the back of his mind as he crossed the cabin, and disintegrated the moment he stepped outside. The roar he'd picked up inside sounded louder out in the thin mountain air. And closer than he'd realized.

Not a truck, he decided after it throttled down for a turn, and then revved up again. Not a car, either. His mouth settled into a tight smile.

He knew that road-eating snarl. Only a Harley XL 883 Custom Sportster chewed up the asphalt and spit it out like that, and Marsh knew exactly who was driving this particular Harley. Deactivating the sensors, he hooked his thumbs in his pockets and waited at the top of the path.

The roar reached crescendo pitch. Gravel scattered. Silence descended. A moment later, his brother stalked up the path. Evan's tawny hair was plastered against his skull from his helmet. Fire blazed in his eyes.

"What the hell do you think you're doing?"

"Good to see you, too," Marsh drawled.

"Listen to me, you hardheaded cowboy. It took me five calls to track you down and seven hours to get here. I'm in no mood for games. Do you have any idea how close you are to crossing the line?"

"I know what I'm doing."

"Do you?" The assistant D.A. slapped the dust from his jeans with an angry palm. "I couldn't believe it when Pepper finally spilled the exact details of your crazy plan."

Marsh hitched a brow. "I see I'm going to have to talk to my partner when I get back to El Paso."

"*If* you get back to El Paso. She's worried about you, dammit, and with good reason. It's not every day a DEA agent kidnaps a potential witness in a federal racketeering case. You're going to have the FBI screaming for your blood."

Marsh didn't point out that the Bureau had been working that particular racketeering case for three years—and that their investigation had gone nowhere, even after Ellen's brutal death. Evan was as frustrated as Marsh by the lack of progress on the case. He'd jerked every string in the Justice Department, just as Marsh had pressured every state and local agency involved in the investigation—until he'd decided to take the investigation on himself.

"I didn't kidnap her," he replied with a shrug. "I simply convinced her it was in her best interests to accompany me."

"Yeah, right! By staging a break-in and scaring the hell out of her."

"I'm definitely going to have a talk with Pepper."

"She didn't tell me about that bit of idiocy," Evan snapped. "I figured it out for myself after I talked to Al Ramos. He told me that someone had busted the locks on Becky Smith's front door right before she agreed to take off with you. I know you, Hoss. I know how you operate. You planned it all out, didn't you? Step by step."

When Marsh didn't reply, his brother's eyes went flat and dangerous.

"You're going to tell me what else you've got up your sleeve, or I swear I'll pound it out of you."

"The last time we exchanged punches, you were fourteen and I was twelve. Think you can still take me?"

"I'll sure as hell give it my best shot."

He might just manage it, too. Evan had kept himself in shape all through law school and the years he'd worked for the Department of Justice. He could still muscle a bawling calf into the chute with the best of them, still spend as many hours in the saddle during fall roundup as any of the Bar-H hands.

"You're not the only one in this, Marsh. We both lost a sister."

The rigidly controlled emotion in his voice struck a chord. Marsh shot a glance over his shoulder. Slanting sunlight cut a swath in front of the cabin, leaving the porch in shadow. They couldn't talk there. Lauren might walk out in the middle of the conversation, and he wasn't ready to explain Evan to her—or last night to Evan.

Hell, he couldn't explain last night to himself. He'd never intended to let things go that far. He'd brought her up here for one reason, and one reason only. He should never have allowed himself to become distracted by her taste, her touch.

Blowing out a long breath, he hooked a thumb toward the side of the cabin. "Let's go over by the woodpile. You can plant your butt on a log while I explain the plan."

After seven hours on the Harley, Evan needed to stretch his legs.

"Just talk. I'll listen."

Marsh plunged in as his brother paced in front of the stacked logs. "David Jannisek is our only link to the shooting. I knew we had to get him in order to get to the man who tried to kill him. All he needed was the proper incentive to come out of hiding."

"Becky Smith—or the woman he thinks is Becky Smith."

"Exactly. So Phase One was to find Ms. Smith."

"And convince her to cooperate by staging that phony break-in."

He nodded. "That was Phase Two."

His nagging guilt took a quantum leap forward with the admission. He'd convinced himself that the ends would justify the means, and that frightening one woman into cooperating was a small enough price to pay for finding another woman's killer. Now...

"Great plan so far," Evan drawled. "A, you find the wrong woman. B, you put your shield at risk to convince her to cooperate. I can't wait to hear Phase Three."

"Phase Three involved getting the word out that I had her."

"The word's out. I heard about it from three different sources down in Tucson. I would have preferred to hear it from my brother," he added, acidly, "but he was pulling his Lone Ranger act."

"I put my job on the line. I wasn't going to put yours, too."

In short, succinct words Evan let him know what he thought about that bit of brotherly concern for his career. He'd picked up a few descriptive adjectives in his dealings with the scum he prosecuted that impressed even the most hardened special agent.

"All right," he growled, once he got that off his chest. "What's Phase Four?"

"That's where it got complicated," Marsh admitted. "I was going to use the time here at the cabin to extract every bit of information I could about Jannisek from Becky."

"Except instead of Becky, you snatched...what's her name? Laurie? Lara?"

"Lauren."

He said her name slowly, remembering his doubts over which sister he'd snared. In retrospect, Marsh couldn't believe he'd mistaken Lauren for her sister, even for a moment. Every report on Becky had painted her as a flighty, flaky tease. Lauren was anything but flaky, and the furthest thing from a tease a man could imagine. She'd given herself completely last night. Held nothing back. Marsh's gut knotted just thinking about those hours on the narrow bunk.

"Lauren," he repeated. "Her name's Lauren."

In the shadows of the porch, Lauren's jaw locked so tight pain shot up the side of her face.

Taut nerves, what seemed like an endless wait, and the sound of deep voices had pulled her outside just moments ago. Just in time to learn that the new arrival was Marsh's brother—and to hear him demand the details of this almighty plan! Anger and hurt piled on top of each other as she listened incredulously.

Marsh had set her up! He'd planned every twist and turn in their convoluted game. She'd run out Becky's back door straight into his arms like a mouse with only one way out of a maze. She'd let him scare her into standing in for her sister. And last night, when she'd cried in his arms and blamed herself for Becky's disappearance, for not trusting him, he'd…he'd just stood there.

Damn him!

"It beats me how you got her to play along with you."

Lauren heard the brother through a haze of fury.

"You tricked her into cooperating. You got her here. You can't drag any information about Jannisek from her, but you somehow manage to convince her to stay and act as the bait you need to trap Jannisek. How did you pull that one off, Hoss? Turn on the famous Henderson charm?"

The silence that followed made Lauren's stomach curl in on itself. Oh, God! He'd planned even those bone-melting kisses? Those hours they'd spent in each other's arms last night?

Part of her refused to believe it. Marsh wasn't capable of that kind of duplicity. Not when he'd held her so close. Not when he'd loved her so wonderfully. But the other part of her, the part fueled by searing anger, called him every name she could think of. She came up with a few choice names for herself while she was at it. How could she have fallen for his line of bull? How could she have let herself be seduced by a pair of laughing blue eyes and a cocky grin?

She didn't wait to hear more. She'd played Marsh's game in a misguided attempt to protect her sister. Despite her efforts, Becky had decided she didn't want her protection and taken off for parts unknown. Marsh could damn well play it alone from here on out.

Seething, Lauren stalked back inside. Her purse she retrieved from the bunk room, the car keys from the table where Marsh had dropped them. It took a severe effort of will not to slam the door behind her when she left.

Her sneakers made no sound on the grass in front of the cabin. She crossed the small clearing, keeping out of sight of the two men still deep in conversation, and hit the path down the hill.

Chapter 11

Immersed in the unfolding plan, Evan watched his brother pace. It still worried him that Marsh had skated so close to the edge in his determined hunt for Ellen's killers, but deep down he shared his frustration.

God knew Evan had worked every angle he could. Ruthlessly, he'd used both his powers of persuasion and the authority of his office to pressure the FBI into putting more resources on the racketeering investigation. Like Marsh, he'd squeezed every source he knew dry. He'd even put a considerable dent in his personal savings to buy information offered by snitches, all of which had led to dead ends. He wanted the man behind the deadly cross fire that had killed Ellen with the same fierce determination his brothers did.

But he wouldn't seduce an innocent woman to get to the killer. Nor would Marsh.

"You're not going to try to convince me you sweet-talked this Lauren into bed as part of your plan, are you?"

Jaw tight, fists shoved in his pockets, Marsh looked ready to take Evan up on his offer to revert back to their rough and tumble boyhood methods for settling disputes.

"Of course not!"

"But you did take her to bed?"

"That's none of your business."

Evan let out a long, slow whistle. Marsh had stepped further over the line than he'd imagined.

"Not smart, Hoss. Not smart at all. You're the last person I'd expect to mix this kind of dangerous business with pleasure."

"Don't you think I know that?" He shoved a hand through his hair. He was as tight as Evan had ever seen him. "The roof could have caved in on me last night and I wouldn't have noticed. And I promised to protect her. Her and her sister. Some protector!"

The searing self-disgust in his voice told its own story. Evidently Marsh was up to his ears in more than a murder investigation. This Lauren Smith seemed to have rocked him right back on his heels.

Good! Someone needed to shake him up. He'd turned too much into himself and his job since his break up with Jenna. A burning desire to meet the woman who could shake the unshakable Marsh gripped Evan.

"Why don't we take this discussion inside? I have a feeling that..."

A distant thud spun both men around.

"What was that?"

Marsh frowned. "I don't know."

A second or two later, the whine of an engine cranking over supplied the answer.

"Someone's departing the premises," Evan observed dryly. "My guess is it's your Lauren."

Marsh took off like a spurred mustang, disappearing around the side of the cabin in three strides. Evan followed. He had one foot on the porch steps when his brother barreled back out the door.

"She's gone." He thrust out a hand. "Give me the keys to your bike."

Marsh caught the keys on the fly and shot down the path, trying to figure why the hell Lauren had bolted. A dozen possibilities raced through his mind as he swung a leg over the Harley's seat, heeled the kickstand, and thumbed the ignition. Maybe the nerve-wracking wait had gotten to her. Maybe last night had shaken her as much as it had shaken him.

Or maybe she'd been feeding him a line of bull all this time about wanting to draw the dogs off her sister's scent. She could have decided to use the diversion of Evan's appearance on the scene to make her escape.

Marsh rejected that possibility instantly. Whatever Lauren's reasons for taking off, she hadn't faked her worry for her sister. Though what the bubble-headed Becky had done to earn that kind of devotion was completely beyond his comprehension at this point. All he knew was that he couldn't let Lauren go without any explanations or any goodbyes.

Or without bringing in Jannisek.

His gut kicked, but the thought of letting Lauren get away dug deeper than the possibility Jannisek might slip through his net. Marsh had let one woman walk out of his life without a protest. True, he'd been in and out of a coma at the time. Yet for reasons he didn't have time to examine at the moment, he was damned if he'd let this one walk out, too.

Bending low over the handlebar, he aimed the Harley down the curving road. The Sportster took the road like the lean, mean, dirt-eating machine it was. Over the engine's roar, he could hear the Blazer up ahead.

Marsh throttled back, leaning into the turns. The pines lining the road blurred into a green haze. Air whipped at his hair and face. The speedometer needle leaped to forty on the flat stretches, dropped to twenty on the turns. He slowed for a hairpin turn and glanced down. Red brake lights flashed through a screen of pines.

After a quick survey of the terrain ahead, he shot off the road, and aimed the Harley down a slope. It was a bumpy ride, but Marsh broke out of the trees and skidded to a stop in the middle of the road just as the Blazer came out of a turn fifty or so yards away.

Swinging off the Sportster, Marsh kicked down the stand, folded his arms and waited. There wasn't room to go around him. She'd have to stop or run right over him.

For a second or two, the issue appeared to be in doubt. He saw her slashing frown. Saw, too, the way she hunched over the wheel. Then the Blazer's brakes squealed. It pitched to a stop a scant ten feet away. His jaw tight, Marsh covered the short distance and wrenched open the driver's door.

"You want to tell me why you took off like that?"

"You want to know? You really want to know? All right. I'll tell you."

She came out swinging. Her leather shoulder bag hit Marsh square in the chest with just enough force to send him stumbling back a pace or two.

"For starters, there's Phase One."

"You heard that?"

"I…" She swung again. "…heard."

Whap!

"Lauren, let me explain."

"Then, there's Phase Two."

Whap!

Marsh took the blow on his upraised arm. "Listen to me…"

"You planned everything, you bastard! Every touch. Every kiss. Even…" Whap! "…last night!"

He protected his head and shoulders, hoping she'd run out of steam before she beat him to a pulp with her purse. What the hell did she have in the thing, anyway?

"And I fell for it!" she raged, winding up for another attack. "Fool, that I am, I fell for it. You'd think I would've learned my lesson by now."

That spurred him to action. He ducked, snagged her wrist as it swung past, and came up in a move that twisted her swinging arm back behind her and brought her up hard against him.

"Let's get one thing straight, right here and right now. Last night wasn't part of any plan. It was a mistake. A stupid, dangerous mistake."

"Oh, that makes me feel *so* much better!"

He was digging the hole deeper with every word and had no idea how to get out.

"Lauren, if you'll just calm down and listen to me...."

"I'm through listening to you. You're a worse liar than my ex-husband, and that takes some doing. Let me go."

"No."

The flat refusal brought her head back. Eyes narrowed, she hissed a warning. "Marsh..."

He tightened his grip. "I lost myself in you last night. Lost sense of everything but you. That's not smart for an agent working a situation."

His mangled explanation didn't appease her. If anything, it incensed her even more.

"I've got news for you, Mr. Hot-Shot Special Agent. It wasn't exactly the smart thing for *anyone* to do. I can't believe I lost all control like that!"

She looked so completely disgusted, so flushed and furious and un-Lauren-like that he wanted to bend her back over his arm and kiss her until they both went blind or crazy or both.

"When this is over," he promised, "I'm going to do my best to make you lose control as often as I can manage it."

"When this is over, I'm never going to see you again!"

"We'll negotiate 'never' when we come to it. In the meantime, I'm asking you to believe me. I didn't make love to you with deliberation and malice aforethought."

"Ha! You never considered it? You never once thought about the possibility or calculated its impact on your precious plan?"

He couldn't lie to her. Not again. "All right, maybe the idea occurred to me."

Her hiss raised the hairs on the back of his neck.

"Making love to you didn't figure into the plan, Lauren, I swear. But from the moment you crashed into me in Becky's backyard, I couldn't get your feel or your scent out of my head. You got in the way of every thought. Every breath I took. The truth is I couldn't stop myself last night. I wanted you so badly I hurt with it. I want you now."

He waited for her protest, bracing for an elbow to the ribs or a knee to the groin. She didn't attempt either. Instead, she leaned back on his arm and studied his face through eyes narrowed to slits.

"I won't deny that I wanted what happened last

night,'' she said finally. "But it won't happen again. Not until we sort this mess out. Maybe not ever again. I don't trust you.''

A knee to the groin would have been easier to take. Too late, Marsh realized the shield he'd built around himself had cracked wide open, leaving him exposed and vulnerable.

Her uncompromising rejection bit into his pride. More disconcerting, the fact that he'd lost something he hadn't known he wanted until that moment started an ache right under his ribs.

He didn't understand how she'd gotten to him this way. He couldn't love her. Hell, he'd known her for all of seventy-two hours. He'd wanted her for seventy-one and a half, sure. What man wouldn't want a vibrant, seductive woman like Lauren? But mere wanting shouldn't cause the irreversible need that seemed to have lodged square in the middle of his chest.

"You're still holding back,'' she said, cutting into his chaotic thoughts. "I want the truth, Marsh. All of it.''

He nodded. It was time. Past time.

"All right. I'll follow you back to the cabin. We'll talk there.''

Evan was waiting for them on the front porch. Boot propped on the railing, he observed their silent progress up the path.

Lauren sailed past him without a word. Marsh followed, hooking his head to indicate that they were taking the discussion inside. The attorney dropped his boot with a thud. "Looks like you've got yourself a hostile witness here, Hoss."

"She overheard our conversation," Marsh muttered. "Or parts of it, anyway. I've got to try and fill in the missing pieces."

"This should be interesting."

Marsh narrowed his eyes. Evan was taking entirely too much enjoyment from the situation. And entirely too much interest in Lauren. His eyes gleamed as he surveyed the rigid figure waiting with arms crossed inside the cabin. A soundless whistle whispered from his mouth.

"I see why you went ahead with your harebrained scheme even after you snatched the wrong sister. She looks like she'd deliver the same kick as Shad's hackberry brandy."

Marsh's muscles did a slow coil. The Henderson brothers had never poached on each other's territory after a claim had been staked. That didn't mean blood hadn't flowed a time or two during the process of sorting out who was going to get to the claim office first.

The idea of smooth, sophisticated Evan making a move on Lauren went a quarter of the way down Marsh's gullet and stuck there.

"Just shut up and let me do the talking."

Eyes mocking, his brother swept out an arm. "Be my guest."

Lauren lifted her chin at their entrance. She'd had time to cool down a little during the brief ride back to the cabin. But only a little. Anger still simmered just below the surface. Hurt still pinged at her.

Marsh's gruff declaration that he'd lost himself with her had lessened that hurt considerably. She'd be the most gullible fool in the world to believe a word he said, but she couldn't deny that her heart had skipped a few beats when he'd bent her back over his arm and threatened to kiss her.

She had that traitorous organ under control now. Or thought she did. The sight of the two Hendersons lined up side-by-side in front of her caused it to skip again. Marsh on his own could make any woman's pulse take off. But with Marsh backed up by a brother with sun-streaked hair, tanned skin and a smile that started slow and finished lazy, the effect was twice as potent and four times more dangerous.

"Lauren, this is my brother Evan. Evan, Lauren Smith."

"Were you part of this scheme, too?" she demanded.

"No, but I'll tell you right up front I want the same end he does."

The answer was smooth and unruffled, and the unspoken message came through loud and clear. He might not agree with his brother's tactics, but the Hendersons would always close ranks when one of their own came under attack.

"Why?" She glanced from one to the other, not understanding what had drawn Evan, as well as Marsh, into this single-minded pursuit. "Why the

heck is it so important to you to nail the man who
tried to take out David Jannisek?''

"He didn't tell you?"

"Tell me what?"

Evan shot his brother a quick, disgusted look.

"No," Marsh ground out. "I didn't tell her."

"Tell me what?"

"Why the hell not?"

A muscle worked on the side of Marsh's jaw. "I
wasn't ready to admit..."

"That you'd gone over the line?"

"What line?" Lauren demanded.

"If you don't tell her, I will."

"Butt out, counselor. This is between Lauren and
me."

This three-way conversation was getting nowhere
fast. With a grunt of exasperation, Lauren stomped
forward, and put herself between the two men.

"I want to hear this from Marsh."

Summarily dismissed by both parties involved,
Evan retired from the field. Lauren didn't even notice when he hauled a kitchen chair around and
straddled it. Her whole attention was riveted on the
man standing still as a statue before her.

"*What* didn't you tell me?"

The muscle in his jaw twitched again. "The shots
intended for Jannisek missed him."

"I know that much. Go on."

His eyes went hard and flat, as though he didn't
want her to glimpse the emotion behind them. He

wouldn't, she thought. He wasn't the kind to let anyone see what he didn't want seen.

"The bullets hit someone else. An innocent victim who just happened to drive through the intersection at the same time Jannisek did."

Lauren's stomach sank. The whole idea of a shooting was frightening enough in the abstract. This was hard, cold reality.

"Who got hit?"

"Our brother Jake's wife."

"Was she…was she badly hurt?"

"She was killed instantly."

Her anger vanished on a wave of sympathy. "Oh, Marsh. I'm sorry."

He didn't seem to want her whispered condolence. What he wanted, she realized with a jolt, was vengeance. So would she if someone had gunned down Becky.

"No wonder you turned the hunt for her killers into a personal quest."

"We all did," Evan said quietly.

Abandoning his chair, he came to stand beside his brother. Once more, the Hendersons closed ranks.

"I put the pressure on everyone I knew in the Justice Department," Evan related. "Our youngest brother, Sam, used his military connections to tap into spook channels. Reece took leave from his job at the Bureau of Land Management to hit the streets with Marsh and shake down every snitch and panhandler in southern Arizona. And that was in addition to the small army of FBI agents who muscled in on the Phoenix PD and took charge of the investigation.''

"With all that, you couldn't pin down the killers?''

"The men who fired the shots disappeared within days of the killing,'' Marsh recounted. "The word on the street is that they paid big time for missing their intended target.''

The hairs on Lauren's arms lifted. Her safe, orderly world seemed a thousand light-years away.

"After that, the leads dried up. Our last hope was Jannisek.''

"And to get to him, you had to get to my sister.''

"Yes.''

She turned and walked away, finally understanding his motivation, yet hurt that he hadn't seen fit to share it with her until it was forced on him. Hugging her arms, she stared into the stone fireplace. It was cold with last night's ashes.

Marsh joined her after a moment. "I'm not apologizing for coercing you into coming with me. I can't. I'd do it again in a heartbeat.''

She didn't answer.

"It was a desperate plan, Lauren, but it was the only one I could come up with.''

"Maybe…maybe I've got a better one.''

She faced him, her heart thumping with the painful realization that he was right. They couldn't let whatever was or wasn't between them interfere with the hunt for this cold-blooded killer.

"You set a trap, but it seems to me you set it for

the wrong prey. If you want the man who engineered your sister's death, you should go after him, not Jannisek.''

''I believe he planned to do just that in Phase Six,'' his brother put in dryly.

''Maybe we can cut out a few steps.''

''What are you thinking?'' Evan asked, moving around Marsh to speak directly to Lauren.

''I'm thinking we don't have the luxury of waiting for Jannisek any longer. My main concern is still to protect Becky, but she could pop up anywhere. Or—'' She swallowed. ''—or the wrong people could find her before we do.''

''We'll find her,'' Marsh promised grimly. ''However long it takes, we'll find her.''

''I don't want to wait. I say we take the offensive.''

''We?'' he echoed, frowning.

''That's right, we.'' Dragging in a deep breath, she plunged into the idea that had been taking shape in her mind. ''We let it leak that Becky knew more about Jannisek's business associates than anyone realized. That she wants to spill everything in exchange for protection. We put out word that he's bringing her back to Phoenix to talk to the authorities. I go in her stead....''

''And certain parties will try to make sure that doesn't happen,'' Evan finished slowly. ''It might work.''

''No!''

The explosive protest jerked their heads around.

"Forget it," Marsh said, flatly. "There's no way I'm setting Lauren up as a target."

She lifted a brow. "Why not? You were eager enough to use me as bait."

"Under controlled conditions, in a place only I knew about, where I could ensure your safety. I'm calling the shots here, and I refuse to put you in the line of fire."

"I have some say in this, too."

"No, you don't."

Red slashed across her cheeks. She'd never met anyone who could take her from anger to hurt to sympathy back to anger again as fast as this man could.

"Let me remind you of a few pertinent facts you seem to have forgotten. One, you dragged me into this. Two, my sister's in danger for as long as this situation goes unresolved. Three, your precious plan hasn't snared your prey. Now I suggest you start treating me as an equal partner in this venture, or…"

A shrill ring swallowed the rest of her angry retort. Evan reached into his shirt pocket for his cellphone. Marsh spun around and grabbed his off the pine table. Both men checked for incoming calls.

With a swift intake of breath, Marsh punched the talk button and jammed the phone to his ear. "Henderson."

His mouth went tight. His gaze cut to Lauren. A moment later, he held out the phone.

"It's your sister. She wants to talk to you."

Chapter 12

The ride down the mountain to the Flagstaff airport was the longest trip of Lauren's life. The road seemed to fold back on itself endlessly. Tall pines blocked any view but the twists ahead. Even the faint scent of vanilla that drifted on the crisp afternoon air failed to distract her for more than a sniff or two. She still hadn't quite absorbed all the ramifications of the call from Becky…or the astounding news that her sister had tracked down David Jannisek and convinced him to put himself in the hands of the authorities.

Nor had Marsh. He wheeled the Blazer with grim intent, eyes locked on the road. He wasn't happy about the fact that Lauren insisted on accompanying him to Palm Springs, where Becky and Dave were

holed up. The air in the line shack had heated like
a blast furnace while he and Lauren debated that
particular detail. What had begun as a terse discussion had quickly degenerated into an argument that
went from professional to personal in a hurry.

When Marsh had couched his concern for her
safety in blunt and highly physical terms, Lauren
had let fly. Evan, of course, had listened with un-
abashed interest as she suggested his brother take
his kisses, his blasted plan and himself straight to
perdition. She was going with him, or she was
damned if she'd tell him where Becky and David
Jannisek were hiding out.

Marsh's response to that outrageous bit of black-
mail had been instant and forceful. To his brother's
considerable amusement, he'd hustled her into the
bunk room and slammed the door. Lauren's mouth
still tingled from his attempts at more direct persuasion.

"A team of FBI investigators will meet us in
Palm Springs," he said curtly, breaking the silence
inside the Blazer. "And Sergeant Al Ramos is flying
in from Phoenix. The feds have jurisdiction on the
racketeering case, but the locals want to run with
their murder investigation."

She nodded, amazed all over again at how her
world had taken on such a sinister tint.

"Our focus is Jannisek," he warned, "but we'll
want some time with Becky, too."

"I won't interfere, if that's what's worrying
you."

He cut her a sideways glance. "You're already interfering."

"How?"

"By making me regret I told Pepper to arrange separate rooms for us in Palm Springs, for starters."

Lauren's stomach clenched. She was regretting it, too, but she hadn't forgotten how Marsh had manipulated her. Or his scathing remarks earlier in the day, for that matter.

"I thought you said making love to me was a mistake. A stupid, dangerous mistake, if I remember correctly."

"It was a mistake…as things stood this morning. The situation's changed, or it will when we get to Palm Springs."

"Then we'll talk about room arrangements when we get to Palm Springs."

They'd talk about more than room arrangements, Marsh vowed. He still hadn't recovered from his gut-twisting reaction to her suggestion that she set herself up as a target. His palms got sweaty just remembering it. He'd lost a sister-in-law to a cold-blooded killer. No way he was going to lose Lauren.

He'd promised her that they'd take up where they left off when this was over. He intended to keep that promise. They had too much unfinished business between them. Like the way she flamed in his arms last night, for starters. And the dryness in his throat when she'd walked out of the bunk room a while ago in the same bottom-hugging jeans, stretchy black knit top and hip-skimming linen jacket she'd worn the night she'd climbed out of a cab in Phoenix.

The diamond unicorn pin winked from her lapel. She'd tamed her hair into a smooth coil that showed off the clean lines of her throat and chin. After several days of seeing her in a baggy sweatshirt—and one long night in nothing at all—Marsh found the switch to this cool, sleek Lauren disconcerting and sexy as all hell.

For the first time since Ellen's death, he wanted the hunt for her killer ended for more reasons than the one that had initially driven him. He wanted to take Lauren out of the darkness he'd plunged her into. He wanted to hear her laughter and watch her skin flush with desire when they made love. Which they would, he swore. After Palm Springs.

His foot pressed down on the accelerator.

They arrived at the Flagstaff airport a half hour later. Marsh picked up their tickets and escorted her to the security checkpoint. Lauren place her carryall on the conveyer while Marsh showed his badge to the senior security checker. After a quiet conversation, he was waved around the checkpoint.

They were halfway down the corridor before she realized he'd been extended more than a professional courtesy. The weapon he'd tucked into its nest at the small of his back would have set off every alarm in the airport. The thought that he might need that lethal automatic in Palm Springs sent a frisson of unease down her spine.

"I didn't think you could carry weapons aboard aircraft," she murmured.

"You can if you're a cop and you call ahead to coordinate the matter with the airlines. It's the pilot's decision."

Evidently this particular pilot had no problems with a gun-toting passenger. The Mesa Airlines flight lifted off a few minutes after Marsh and Lauren boarded and banked into a turn, circling the spectacular San Francisco Peaks. Although she knew it was futile, Lauren searched the tree-covered slopes for a glimpse of the line shack. It was there somewhere, nestled amid those fragrant pines.

The flight from Flagstaff to the desert watering hole of Palm Springs, California, took less than an hour. As the small plane circled before landing, Lauren got a bird's-eye view of sparkling aqua pools in what seemed like every second or third backyard. Surrounding the tile-roofed stucco estates and resorts were more golf courses than she could count.

How like David Jannisek to hide out in a place like this, she thought cynically. Up to his ears in debt and on the run from would-be killers, he wasn't about to abandon his luxurious life-style. Not for the first time, she wondered why in the world Becky had gone to find him. Lauren had brushed aside her sister's breathless explanation over the phone. Beck might think she loved him, but the truth was she fell in and out of love as often as most people changed their underwear.

The thought caused Lauren to squirm in her seat.

The first thing she intended to do after a long heart-to-heart with her sister was hit the shops. She'd decided to forswear her usual sensible nylon briefs and bras in favor of something a bit more risqué, but these blasted thongs had to go.

Resolutely, Lauren kept her eyes on the dazzling scenery below. She wasn't about to admit that Marsh's unconditional approval of Becky's taste in undergarments had influenced her decision to refurbish her own wardrobe. At this point, she wasn't ready to admit anything concerning Marsh Henderson.

She'd never met anyone who could rouse her to such equal parts anger and passion. In fact, now that her temper had cooled, she could admit she'd never met anyone like Marsh, period.

For the first time since she'd agreed to accompany him into protective custody in Becky's stead, she wanted this whole, awful business over with for reasons that had nothing to do with her sister's safety. The sooner Marsh completed his quest, the sooner they could figure out just where this undeniable attraction between them was going.

The hand he rested at the small of her back while they waited to deplane told her this magnetism had to go somewhere. She could feel his touch right through her linen jacket.

They stepped off the plane into a desert heat that made Lauren long instantly for Arizona's mountains. Fall hadn't hit this playground of the rich and famous yet. The tall palms that gave the watering hole its name thrust up against a searing blue sky.

Despite the heat, the man who met them outside the terminal wore a dark suit. Lauren didn't figure out why until he reached courteously for her carryall and flashed a leather shoulder strap under his coat. Like Marsh, he was armed.

The unease that had gripped her at the Flagstaff airport returned with a vengeance.

She sat silently in the back seat of the sedan their escort had waiting at the curb. He filled the short drive with a casual commentary, pointing out the streets named after the town's most prominent denizens. With Marsh taut and silent beside her, Lauren couldn't summon the least interest in Hope, Autry, Sinatra or Shore Street.

Her prickling unease vaulted into distinct nervousness when they turned into a sprawling resort and walked into the casita where David Jannisek had been living for the past few weeks under an assumed name. What looked like a small army of law enforcement officials had descended on the place.

Marsh seemed to know most of them. He was performing introductions when a glad cry rang through the room.

"Lauren!"

Becky tumbled out of the adjoining bedroom, her face alight with relief and joy. The sisters met in a fierce hug. They were both near tears when they pulled apart.

"Oh, Beck, I was so worried about you!"

"You gave me a few hairy moments, too." Sniffling, she tucked a stray strand behind Lauren's ear. "You practically disappeared off the face of the earth. Where were you?"

"In a shack in the mountains."

Becky's irrepressible spirits returned with a hiccup of laughter. "Well, I guess if we both had to go into hiding, I'm glad you got the shack and I got Palm Springs."

"Thanks!"

The laughter faded almost as quickly as it had come. "Can you stay for a few days, Laur? Please. Just until we get this mess sorted out and I know what's going to happen next?"

Lauren didn't hesitate. Josh and her business would just have to wait another few days. She couldn't go off and leave Becky in this crisis.

Or Marsh.

She buried that thought quickly with a smiling assent. "Sure, I can stay. Are you all right?" she asked quietly, noting the bluish shadows under Becky's eyes.

"I will be, when this is over. Come on, I want to hear every detail."

There were a few details Lauren wanted to hear, too, but first things first. She tugged her sister around to face the man watching them from a few feet away.

"This is Special Agent Marsh Henderson."

"Well, well," Becky murmured, her voice dropping into the teasing lilt that came as natural to her as breathing. "I might not have skipped town if I'd known you were waiting to whisk me off to a mountain hideaway."

Lauren couldn't be jealous. She absolutely refused to dig her nails into Becky's arm. But that didn't stop her from feeling a spurt of satisfaction when Marsh appeared unaffected by her sister's thorough and very appreciative appraisal. His face registered only a thoughtful interest as he studied first one sister, and then the other.

"I know," Becky said, with a wicked grin. "Most people can't tell us apart."

His eyes shifted to Lauren. A half smile tugged at his mouth. "That's a mistake I'll only make once."

The effervescent Becky blinked, not quite sure how to take that. She recovered quickly, however.

"Henderson?" she mused. "Henderson? Where have I heard that name?"

"It was in all the Phoenix papers six weeks ago," a thin, handsome Hispanic put in from the other side of the room. Al Ramos, Lauren guessed. The Scottsdale homicide detective in charge of the murder investigation, according to Marsh.

"Ellen Henderson was the woman who took the bullets intended for David Jannisek," he told Becky.

The color drained from her cheeks. Her stricken gaze flew from the detective to Marsh. "Oh, no! Was she a relation?"

"My sister-in-law."

"I'm sorry," she whispered.

He nodded, obviously unwilling to display his private grief in public. Then he got right to the business that had consumed him for all these weeks. "Where's Jannisek?"

"Out on the patio, talking to some FBI agents."

He turned without another word and made for the glass doors.

"Wait! They said they didn't want to be interrupted."

"Tough."

Becky blinked again, and turned to Lauren with a wry smile. "A man of few words, I see. Was he that uptight the whole time you were together at that shack?"

"He had his moments."

She should have known her sister's inner antennae were too finely tuned to any and all things male to accept that response at face value.

"No kidding? Did he try to come on to you or something?"

"Becky!"

"Laur, you're blushing!" Ignoring the other occupants in the room, none of whom made the least pretense of minding his own business, she gave a little hoot. "He did! Well, I'll be darned. He put the make on you!"

Her face flaming, Lauren dragged at her sister's arm. "Let's go somewhere where we can talk. In private."

Before abandoning the room, Becky shot another glance over her shoulder at Marsh. Her appraising glance started with his wide shoulders and swiftly traveled south. Her eyes danced by the time she closed the bedroom door behind them.

"To each her own, sister of mine. But I speak from vastly superior experience when I tell you you're going to have your hands full with that one."

"Never mind my hands. What about yours?"

Lauren pushed a jumble of glossy magazines, frothy underwear and discarded clothing off one corner of the bed. Becky certainly hadn't wasted any time making herself comfortable in the luxurious suite. Dragging her sister down beside her, Lauren demanded the explanations that were so late in coming.

"How did you get tangled up with someone like David Jannisek?"

Her sister's laughter died, and in its place came an expression Lauren never remembered seeing on her face before. She looked completely unsure of herself.

"It started off as a fling. One of my usual love 'em and ditch 'em relationships. But he's so charming and extravagant and darned sexy."

"He almost *charmed* you right into the middle of a shoot-out."

"I know," Becky said miserably. "I couldn't believe it when the police knocked on the door and told me what happened. They asked me all kinds of questions. And then Dave disappeared. I told myself I was well rid of him, but..."

"But what?"

She pleated the colorful bedspread with restless fingers. "But it hurt, Laur. More than I expected it to. Sometime between the silly jokes and the extravagant gifts, I fell for the jerk. Big time."

"Oh, no!"

"I didn't want to. I tried like the dickens to put him out of my mind. I was going to camp out with you in Denver for a few weeks while I got my head straight again. Then you called and told me hunky Henderson out there intended to use me as bait to lure Dave out of hiding. I couldn't let him walk blindly into a trap. I had to talk to him first." She gave her sister a wobbly, un-Beckyish smile. "I knew as soon as I saw him again that I...I love him."

Lauren's heart sank. Her laughing, frivolous sister had never come close to loving before. How like her to finally fall for exactly the wrong man.

"How did you find him?"

"I had a hunch he'd come here." Her glance drifted around the lavish suite. "He said he'd spent the happiest days of his life in Palm Springs...with me."

"Oh, that's original."

The sardonic retort brought a smile, less wobbly this time. Becky's response cut right through the disdain Lauren felt toward the hotelier, sight unseen.

"He's had a rough time, Laur. His wife died in a car crash just a year after they were married. They were in their last year of college, and Dave could never afford to buy her anything, even a wedding ring. I think that's how he lost all sense of value where money's concerned—and why he spent so much on me.''

"Not just on you." Lauren unclasped the unicorn pin. "This has to go back."

"He wanted you to have it. *I* wanted you to have it.''

"I can't keep it." She folded her sister's fingers over the pin. "It's too expensive. You shouldn't have let him buy it."

"I know," Becky agreed glumly. "It's just that Dave has this need to give. He won't admit it, but his generosity comes straight from the heart. He flashes this sexy smile and charms the pants off you, but underneath he's…he's…''

Her hand lifted, dropped.

"…he's one of a kind." She slid a glance at Lauren. "Kinda like your special agent."

"He's not *my* special agent."

Like sunshine piercing through a cloud, Becky's laughter returned. "Ha! I saw the look he gave you when he made that crack about not confusing the two of us again. Come on, girl, spill it. Tell me you put all that raw male and hard muscle to good use."

Lauren couldn't dodge the pointed question. Her sister knew her too well.

"It was a mistake. A moment of sheer insanity. We were alone and things got tense…''

"I'll bet!"

"…and it just sort of…happened."

"Oh, that's original," Becky teased, throwing the

words back at her. "So what's the story? Are you
going to let things just sort of happen again?"

It was Lauren's turn to pleat the colorful bedspread. "I don't know."

"Do you want to?"

"Yes. Maybe." She heaved an exasperated sigh.
"I don't know. Up to a point, he was only interested
in how I fit into his plan to hunt down the man
behind the attack on David. Now...I just don't
know."

"Trust me," her sister said with all the confidence
of a woman who knew whereof she spoke, "he's
interested in you for reasons that have nothing to do
with any plan."

Lauren wanted to believe her, almost as much as
she wanted to believe that she and Marsh would pick
up where they'd left off after this was all over. But
she wasn't sure she liked being slotted into one part
of his life, and shut out from others.

Right now, he considered her a distraction, a dangerous one at that. Intellectually, Lauren could accept that. She even harbored a grudging respect for
his single-minded determination to bring the man
behind his sister-in-law's death to justice. What she
was having difficulty accepting was the emotional
wall he seemed to put between the hunt and everything else in his life—now including her.

That feeling of separation increased over the long
hours that followed. Marsh and the rest of the team
grilled David Jannisek relentlessly. By late after-

noon, Becky had been drawn into the process, as well. Although she'd never been formally introduced to many of David's so-called associates, she'd seen him talking to them on several occasions. Having her sister's eye for detail, she provided descriptions to a crime analyst to feed into a laptop computer.

Lauren hung around the casita for most of the day, feeling useless. Later that evening, the team finally let Jannisek and Becky take a break while they remained huddled on the patio together to discuss what they'd gathered so far.

Over an ordered-in dinner of pizza and soft drinks, Lauren finally met her sister's David face-to-face. He was every bit as charming as Lauren had expected, and devastatingly handsome. With his tanned skin, tawny hair and Clark Gable-style mustache, he needed only the ascot and jodhpurs to complete his aristocratic image. Even in loafers, tan slacks and a black knit shirt, he looked as though he'd walked right out of the pages of *GQ*.

But it was his bone-deep regret for having drawn Becky into the pit he'd dug for himself that won Lauren's grudging approval. That, and his determination to make what restitution he could.

"I'm going to pay back everything I owe," he said quietly, tapping his ring finger on the table in a steady, unconscious rhythm. "I piled up too many legitimate debts as a result of my gambling."

Becky reached across the table to squeeze his hand.

"Marsh says the information Dave's providing is payment enough to society," she told her sister, "but he won't listen."

Surprised, Lauren sifted through the figures on the patio for the man who'd hunted Jannisek so ruthlessly. Concentration etched a deep groove in Marsh's forehead. His black hair gleamed in the light of the ceramic lanterns decorating the walled-in patio. In jeans and rolled-up shirtsleeves, he looked tough and uncompromising and not at all the kind of predator who would show this sympathy toward his prey.

"Hopefully, the information I'm giving him will lead to the man he wants."

She dragged her attention back to Dave, whose own attention was focused exclusively on her sister.

"If it does," he told a subdued Becky, "it'll be months, maybe years, before the case comes to trial."

Dismay put a squeak in her voice. "Years?"

"They want to put me in the witness protection program. It means a new name, a new life." His hand tightened around hers. "I can't take you with me. I won't expose you to that kind of danger again. After the trial, when the man who wants me dead is put away, I'll come looking for you."

Her mouth curved in an attempt at a smile. "I suppose you think I'll be waiting."

"No! I don't have any right to ask you to put your life on hold. I'll come for you. If you haven't found someone else, maybe we can start again."

She swallowed. "Maybe."

He hooked a finger under her chin. Lauren could only guess at what it cost him to keep his voice even and his eyes gentle on Becky's face.

"Someday you'll bump into this stranger and he'll flash a smile at you that will turn your world upside down." His thumb stroked a pattern on Becky's chin. "It'll be like the first time, baby, only in reverse. Remember how your saucy grin blew me away when I walked into the lounge to check out the new cocktail waitress?"

"I remember."

"A few years from now, I'll walk up to you on the street or in some restaurant or shopping mall and you won't know what hit you."

Becky's throat worked. "Maybe."

Neither of them noticed when Lauren took her soft drink and slipped away. She ached for her sister, but knew in her heart this was one problem she couldn't jump in and fix for her.

Feeling more extraneous than ever, she retired to her own casita next to Becky and Dave's. It was furnished in the same luxurious mix of Impressionistic colors and Southern California chic, with Monet prints on the walls and a bedroom dominated by a Sonoma-style, wrought iron four-poster bed draped in twisted grapevines and romantic, billowing sheers. As she surveyed the sybaritic creation, she couldn't help comparing it to the narrow bunk she and Marsh had tumbled into last night.

At the thought, desire whipped like prairie fire

through her veins. With an intensity that shook her, she longed to share that football-field-sized bed with Marsh.

Watching Becky and Dave tonight had brought home again how fragile this absurd condition called love was. One minute, your heart sang and you were talking about forevers. The next, you might find yourself riddled with regrets.

No! Not this time!

Whatever happened between her and Marsh, she decided fiercely, there wouldn't be any regrets.

She slid between cloud-soft cotton sheets with renewed resolve to hit some of Palm Springs' exclusive boutiques first thing in the morning. She might not have a clue if or when they'd pick up where they'd left off at the cabin, but she wanted to be prepared in either case.

Chapter 13

To Lauren's disappointment, Marsh nixed her proposed shopping expedition the next morning. Until the team finished with Dave, he thought it best for everyone concerned to keep a low profile.

As a result, she was forced to raid Becky's wardrobe yet again. She found a soft, cottony V-necked tank in shell pink to wear with her jeans. Her sister insisted that she also take the flesh-colored Wonderbra that transformed the plain little top into a seductive showcase of feminine charms.

Lauren felt self-conscious about her dramatically altered curves all day, not that anyone saw them but her. Marsh remained huddled with Dave and the rest of the team all morning and well into the afternoon. Lauren didn't see him until later that evening, when he knocked on her door.

He looked both tired and elated at the same time, she thought, like a man nearing the end of a long quest. But evidently he wasn't too tired to notice the way she filled the V-necked sweater. His gaze slid south and snagged there for a moment or two, but he nobly refrained from comment. Instead, he smiled at her with a warmth that made her heart thump erratically under her borrowed clothing.

"It's been a helluva two days. I've missed you."

Her brow lifted. He'd been so intent and focused on his mission, she didn't think he'd remembered she was still in Palm Springs, much less missed her.

"That's good. I think."

His gaze drifted to her mouth. "It's good."

Ridiculously flustered by that sort-of declaration, she invited him in.

"Have you finished with Dave?"

"Just about." He strolled into the spacious living room and sank down beside her on the elegant, tapestry-covered sofa. "Jannisek's given us enough information to mount a five-state raid within the next few weeks. Even more important, he put a face and a name to the man who sicced those hired guns on him. Henry Mullvane."

The steely satisfaction in his voice told Lauren it wouldn't be long before Mr. Mullvane was breathing in recirculated prison air.

"Henry Mullvane doesn't sound like a very mobsterish name."

"You were expecting maybe Luciano or Corleone?"

"Well..."

"Times have changed. Some of the worst criminals today own legitimate businesses, are members of the Chamber of Commerce and sit on the school board. Our boy Mullvane runs a nationwide chain of appliance stores."

Marsh was right. Times had changed. Somehow Lauren had trouble envisioning a cold-blooded killer worried about retail sales of refrigerators and stoves. Curling her legs under her, she leaned an elbow on the sofa-back and threaded a hand through her hair.

"Dave told Becky and me last night that it could be months before this guy comes to trial."

"Or longer. When we finish here, which we expect to do by tomorrow afternoon, we'll bust his home and his corporate headquarters in Phoenix. What we find there could keep us busy for years."

Lauren remembered his brother's scathing remarks about Marsh overstepping his authority and coming too damned close to crossing the line.

"I thought the DEA wasn't officially involved in this investigation."

A wolfish grin slashed across his face. "It is now. My boss practically salivated when I passed on the information Dave gave us about Mullvane's connections to the South American drug cartels."

It was obvious that Marsh's single-minded determination to bring his sister-in-law's killer down wouldn't terminate with the man's apprehension. He'd follow this case through to the end, no matter how long it took.

Lauren felt a stab of empathy for Becky, who'd been quiet and subdued all day. Like Dave, Marsh could remain tied up in this tangle for years. So could this uncertain, ephemeral…something…that shimmered between Marsh and Lauren. The realization left a hollow feeling in her chest.

"If you're wrapping things up here tomorrow afternoon, I'll head back to Denver. Becky, too. She's going to stay with me for a while."

"She told me." He hesitated. "It looks to me as though she's got it as bad for Jannisek as he does for her."

"I'm beginning to think so, too."

An indefinite wait for a man who hadn't yet proven himself worth waiting for wasn't what Lauren would wish for her sister, but then it wasn't her choice to make. She stopped thinking about Becky when Marsh reached out to slide a hand through her hair. Warm fingers encircled her nape. His thumb stroked a line along her jaw.

"I don't know how long it'll take us to mount this raid on Mullvane's operations, but after that…"

"Yes?"

"I'm thinking it's been a while since I've been to Denver."

Lauren's heart seemed to stop in her chest. She barely got it going again when he added a kicker.

"I'm also thinking that we said we were going to talk about room arrangements when we got to Palm Springs."

He gave her a look that managed to be both hopeful and aggrieved.

"You might want to know that I spent most of last night with Jannisek, and what was left of it thinking about you. I told you you'd interfere."

His thumb made a slow circle on her cheek.

"I'm damned if I know how you got under my skin in such a short time, but you have."

As declarations went, it was a little short on romance but long on impact. The wall Lauren had felt growing between them for the past two days crumbled.

"Any chance we could rekindle the fire we started at the cabin? Maybe it could keep us both warm until I get to Denver."

She wasn't about to tell him that his touch had already set a spark to the flames.

"Maybe," she murmured.

He took that as an assent and leaned forward another inch. Their mouths met, fitting together as naturally as two pieces of a jigsaw puzzle. His touch was warm, his taste all Marsh. Lauren could swear she caught a hint of vanilla on his lips. She smiled, thinking she'd always associate him with ice cream and tree bark. Then he drew her into his lap, and she swept right past thinking into need.

He cradled her in one arm, palmed her hip with the other. She slid her hands up the muscled planes of his chest to wrap around his neck. Their mouths met, hers as hungry as his. With a rush of greed, she surged up against him.

"Ouch!"

He jerked away as if stung.

"What?" She crashed back to reality a gasp. "What did I do?"

"You didn't do it." Grimacing, he reached into his shirt pocket. "This thing did. I guess I didn't close the darned clasp."

He opened his fist. The prancing, diamond-studded unicorn lay in his palm.

"I forgot. I meant to give this to you when I first knocked on your door, but...something distracted me."

She knew darn well what had distracted him. Her pushed-up curves. They seemed to be doing it again. His gaze roamed from the jeweled piece to an appropriate spot to pin it and got stuck somewhere in the middle.

"I don't want the pin," she protested. "I told Dave and Becky it had to go back."

"Yeah, well, Becky wanted you to have it and I figured Jannisek needed a jump start on his climb out of debt. I told him I'd buy this from him."

If Lauren hadn't already suspected that she'd fallen for this rough-edged special agent, his extraordinary generosity to a man who didn't deserve it would have erased her lingering doubts. Her heart contracted, swift and tight, and then expanded with a rush of emotion she didn't quite have the nerve to call love.

"Marsh, I can't accept this. It cost more than two thousand dollars."

"You're worth it."

The smile in his blue eyes made her stomach hollow. It hollowed even more when he jiggled her to a sitting position and tucked his fingers inside the V neck of her sweater. Brows knit in concentration, he wove the pin through the soft cotton and fumbled with the clasp.

It proved too small or too stubborn for his big fingers. His frown deepened. Accidentally or otherwise, his knuckles brushed against her Wondercurves. A slight sweat sheened his forehead by the time he got the pin attached to the sweater.

"Are you okay?" she asked solicitously.

"No! What the heck have you got on under there?"

"Since you didn't want me to hit the shops, Becky insisted I borrow some of her things."

Marsh gave a sound halfway between a growl and a groan. "I seem to remember swearing to keep my hands off you until this was over and we could sort things out between us calmly and sensibly."

"I seem to recall making the same promise."

"I'm not feeling particularly calm or sensible at this moment."

Sighing, she leaned forward to rest her forehead against his. She'd always been the practical sister. The one who set schedules, kept her nose to the grindstone, checked off each goal as she achieved it. The one time she'd followed her heart she'd been burned. Badly.

But this time…

This time the risks were far greater. So were the rewards. As furious as Marsh could make her, he could also take her to dizzying, sensual heights she'd never dreamed of.

Her body had already tightened in anticipation of reaching those same heights again. Need held her in a hard grip. The need to hold him. To feel him inside her. To love him.

"Funny," she whispered, "I'm not feeling particularly calm or sensible right now, either."

"Good!" He erupted from the sofa with Lauren hefted high in his arms. "I told myself that I could walk out of here without seeing what you've got on under that sweater. I lied."

Seeing her in her borrowed undies might have been his original intent when he swept her into the bedroom. Getting her out of them soon constituted a much higher priority.

With his mouth holding hers, his hands went to work stripping her down to the flesh-colored lace.

"Nice."

He dropped a kiss on the swell of her breast, another deep in her impressive cleavage. With the prickly beginnings of his beard rasping against her skin, Lauren resolved to empty her drawers of all nonwired, un-Wonderbras the moment she got home.

"Very nice."

He shaped her with his hands, explored her with his tongue, worshiped her. In a slow spiral of delight, she did the same. Her fingers fumbled with the buttons on his shirt, and then slid through the crisp hair of his chest. His muscles jumped under her touch. Hers clenched with need.

Within moments they were both slick and hot and driven by an urgency that made even her bra and skimpy briefs superfluous. Gasping with pleasure, she shimmied out of what remained of her clothes and helped him do the same. He took time only to sheathe himself before he rolled onto his back and lifted her astride his hips.

Lauren's throat went dry. The artist in her ached with the perfection of his sleek lines, smooth skin and corded muscle. The woman in her cried for the pain he must have suffered from that bullet to the chest.

Artist and woman came together in a rush of plea-sure when she raised her hips and took him into her. They moved slowly at first, each contorting to ex-plore the other without breaking the deliberate, erotic rhythm. Bending, clenching, gasping, Lauren ran her tongue along his jaw and gave her hands free rein. Marsh did the same before he splayed his palms around her waist and surged upward.

With that thrust, slow exploded into fast. With the next, fast spun out of control. A panting eternity later, Lauren arched her back. A cry ripped from her throat as her climax started tight and burst loose.

Marsh waited until her shuddering spasms died, then buried his hands in her hair, dragged her down for a savage kiss, and thrust into her again.

* * *

He rolled out of bed just after dawn and hit the shower. Wearing only a towel and a grin, he strolled out of the bathroom some time later and dropped a kiss on her bare shoulder.

"I'll come back as soon as we wind things up with Jannisek."

"Mmm," she muttered into the pillow.

"This afternoon," he breathed against her bare skin. "Save this afternoon for me."

Lauren pried open one eye to watch him pull on his clothes. Even in her state of mindless, boneless lethargy, the swirl of dark hair around his belly button caused a stir deep in her tummy.

"I'll save this afternoon," she murmured, "but I have to go home tonight. I can't leave things in limbo with my assistant any longer, or I won't have a business."

Fully clothed, he dropped onto the bed beside her. A big, gentle hand brushed her hair from her eyes.

"I'll make time for us, Lauren. The next weeks and months are going to get crazy, but I'll make that trip to Denver as soon as I can."

She sank back into sleep with his promise curled around her heart.

The phone woke her again some hours later. Wincing at its shrill ring, she kept her face buried in the pillow and groped blindly beside the bed.

"Yes?"

"Are you awake, Laur?"

"I am now."

She squinted at her watch, but couldn't make out the digits with eyes still blurred from sleep.

"What time is it?"

"Almost ten."

Ten! She couldn't remember the last time she'd slept past seven or seven-thirty. Of course, she couldn't remember the last time she'd burned up every molecule of energy in such wild abandon, either.

"They're through with me," Becky said. "Do you want to go down to the pool and soak up some rays?"

Pushing upright, Lauren shoved her hair out of her eyes. "Did Marsh say it was safe for you to show yourself in public?"

"He said it was okay as long as one of the men goes down to the pool with us. I thought maybe we could talk."

"Tell you what. I'm a long way from being presentable. Why don't you go on down? I'll join you in a half hour or so and we'll talk away."

"Sounds good to me. See you there."

Lauren hung up and rolled out of bed. She had a good idea what Becky wanted to talk about. The forced cheerfulness in her sister's voice didn't fool Lauren. For the first time in her life, her sister had fallen in love. Now, the man she wanted was preparing to put her out of his life for months, maybe years.

A guilty joy that Marsh didn't intend to do the same snaked through Lauren. His promise to come up to Denver as soon as he could bubbled through her as she twisted the shower taps and waited for the water to heat.

She didn't even try to deny anymore that she loved him. All her arguments against such an improbable, impossible happening had gone up in flames last night. And again this morning, when he'd dropped both a kiss and that promise on her. Hugging the memory of both to her, she stepped into the glass enclosure.

Thirty minutes later, she finished blow-drying her hair. It took another ten to put on her makeup, but only one to decide what to wear. She hadn't packed a bathing suit for her hurried trip to Phoenix. Her faithful jeans and the borrowed pink sweater would have to do.

Smiling, she fingered the sparkling unicorn still pinned to the cloud-soft cotton. Strange how the little creature had figured so prominently in the unfolding drama that included Becky, Dave, her and Marsh.

Not ten minutes later, it played another, even more dramatic role.

With the desert heat dry against her bare arms, Lauren walked through the series of shaded courtyards that led to the pool. She could hear the splashing of the dolphin fountain around the next turn when a waiter in a white jacket with the resort's logo on the breast pocket hailed her.

"Ms. Smith?"

"Yes?"

"I have a message for you."

Wondering if Becky had changed her mind about their meeting spot, Lauren turned with smile. "Yes?"

A second man stepped out of the shadows. Short and pudgy, he wore a dark suit and an air of ruthless determination.

Lauren's smile wavered, and then disintegrated completely as the waiter reached into his jacket and withdrew a gun topped with a long, deadly silencer. Before she could so much as gasp, let alone turn and flee, he grabbed her. With one hand wrapped viciously around her arm, he jammed the barrel into her side.

"You make one sound, one single sound, and you're dead."

With her throat closed and her heart slamming against her ribs, she couldn't have squeaked out a word if she wanted to.

"You sure we got the right broad?" the second man growled. "I seen another one with her color hair by the pool."

"Yeah, I'm sure. Look at the piece of ice she's wearing. I saw the receipts for that pin when we trashed Jannisek's place."

Again! It was happening again! These creeps had mistaken her for Becky.

"Wait! You... Oh!"

The gun barrel jabbed hard into Lauren's side, cutting off her instinctive protest. She stumbled, breathless with pain. The hand on her arm wrenched her upright.

"Don't make me hurt you," her abductor snarled. "We need you breathing for a while, but that don't mean we need you walking."

Her jaw clamped shut. She wasn't going to send these creeps after her sister. Heart thundering, she was half dragged, half shoved toward a car idling at the back of the building. The sedan's motor hummed softly. Its dark tinted windows revealed nothing of its interior.

Lauren's abductor jerked her to a halt.

His accomplice performed a swift reconnaissance of the open parking lot, and then dashed to the car and yanked open the back door.

Seconds later, Lauren was shoved into the back seat.

Chapter 14

Lauren fell into the seat, numb with disbelief. For the second time in less than two weeks, she'd been mistaken for her sister. But this time, her terror-filled mind screamed as the car peeled away from the curb, the consequences might just prove fatal.

She scrambled upright and eyed the door handle only inches away. If she could knock aside the gun aimed at her middle with her right hand and yank the door open with her left, she could tumble into the street and...

"Don't try it, babe."

The man beside her smiled a warning.

"Me or my friend here would put a bullet through your kneecap before you ran two steps."

He said it with such casual menace that ice formed in Lauren's veins.

"But just to make sure…" In a swift move, he caught her wrist in a brutal grip and twisted it behind her. "Joey, toss me that tape."

Bent almost double, Lauren fought futilely as he laid his gun on the seat and snagged her other arm. She heard a tearing sound, and then felt the slap of tape as he wrapped it around and around her wrists. Panting, she lurched back in her seat.

"You can't do this!"

The man in the front seat snickered. "Looks to me like we just did."

"Shut up and drive, Joey."

Shaking her hair out of her eyes, Lauren bit back the terror that rose like a living thing in her throat. She had to rein in her thundering fear. Had to focus. Breathing hard and fast, she tried to identify landmarks she could relate to Marsh when she got the chance. She *would* get the chance. When they arrived wherever they were going, she'd find some way to contact him or send a message.

He was a hunter. He'd track these thugs down and come after her. She had to believe that, had to keep shouting it over and over in her mind to keep from choking on the panic pounding through her chest.

With every turn, she searched for street signs. She recognized Sinatra Avenue and caught a glimpse of the boutiques and restaurants lining the main street she'd wanted to stroll down yesterday. All too soon, the familiar landmarks blurred. After a confusing number of turns, they wheeled into a neighborhood of towering palms, profusely flowering shrubs and high walls.

The streets grew wider, the residences separated into estates. Finally, the driver slowed at a gated driveway. A "For Sale" sign beside the entrance offered the property for viewing to a discriminating clientele.

Evidently her abductors had arranged a private viewing. With a click of a remote switch, the gates slid open. Crushed shell crunched under the tires as the car swept up a curving drive to a sprawling stucco mansion. Its red tile roof had aged to a deep ocher. The ornate curlicues above the windows and massive front doors dated it somewhere in the thirties or forties. Lauren couldn't imagine who owned it, but they had to be one of Palm Springs' wealthiest celebrities or billionaires.

It soon became obvious that the owners had departed the premises. The front doors opened to cavernous rooms emptied of all furnishings. The place was in show condition, however. The black-and-white marble floors gleamed. The massive crystal chandelier in the entryway sparkled. Not a speck of dust danced in the sunbeams slanting through the curtained front windows.

With a hand wrapped around her arm like a vise, Lauren was guided down a long, central hall to the high-ceilinged sunroom that ran the length of the back of the house. Its tall windows looked out on a marble pool surrounded by larger-than-life white statuary and acres of green lawn. The estate's high stucco wall enclosed it all, like the walls of an impregnable fortress.

Sliding open the glass doors, her kidnapper took her into the bright sunshine. Like the interior, the exterior was meticulously maintained. No weeds poked out of the lush green carpet. No algae had dared form on the sides of the pool. A well-mannered hum rose from the pool's motor, neatly concealed behind a latticework screen. Chlorine mingled with the scent of bougainvillea and honeysuckle.

"Over there."

Following the curt instruction, she made her way to a grotto formed by a half circle of Greek columns. Climbing vines shaded the grotto's interior, which held a grouping of marble benches and tables.

"Damned place ain't got no place to sit but out here," the one called Joey muttered. "Next time, we tell that pansy-assed Realtor friend of the boss's to pick a joint with chairs and a TV in it, for God's sake."

Disgusted, he whipped a cigarette pack out of his pocket and lit up.

"You might as well sit down," he grumbled to Lauren. "We got some time to kill yet."

Lauren sank onto a marble bench, her wrists still taped and her shoulders already aching from the strain. She swallowed, trying desperately to work some moisture in her throat.

"Some time until what?"

"Until your boyfriend takes a one-way ride out into the desert," he answered, carelessly.

She must have made some sound. A moan or a little cry. The older one, the one whose gun had bruised her ribs, snarled a warning.

"Shut the hell up, Joey."

"Hey, I was only answerin' her question."

"You got a mouth on you that won't quit, you know that?" Shaking his head, the older man shot back his sleeve to check his watch. "I'm going to get things set up. I'll contact you when it's time to make the call. Got the phone?"

The younger man patted his breast pocket. "I got it."

"Okay. Keep an eye on her."

Joey flicked her a dismissive glance. "She ain't goin' nowheres."

"Just to make sure, tape her ankles." Digging a roll of white tape out of his pocket, he tossed it to his partner and strode off.

When the pudgy Joey sauntered toward her, Lauren coiled her muscles. If the bastard got within kicking range, he was going down hard. To her crushing disappointment, he stopped a pace or two away and eyed her through a curl of cigarette smoke.

"You try anything with me, doll, and I'll put you out cold. Cross your ankles and lift 'em. Come on, lift 'em."

The vague idea that she could bring her knees up into his chin disappeared the moment Lauren lifted her legs. The angle was wrong. She couldn't get any leverage at all, and nearly tumbled off the bench when he grabbed her ankles and banded them with tape. Hiding her frustration and fear, she shot him a look of utter loathing.

Chuckling, he let her feet drop. They hit the marble with a thunk. "Come on, doll! You didn't think the boss was going to let Jannisek rat on him, did you?"

"But…"

She was about to tell him they were too late, that Dave had already told everything he knew. The abrupt realization that she'd make herself expendable with that revelation froze her into silence.

As it turned out, she didn't have to tell him anything. He guessed her thoughts with terrifying accuracy.

"You're thinking that he's already spilled his guts, ain't you? That we took too long getting here?"

She didn't answer, but the garrulous mobster didn't seem to need encouragement. Shaking another cigarette out of his pack, he lit it with the stub of the first. The butt flew in a glowing arc across the grotto.

"We didn't know where he was until we heard 'bout all the feds convergin' on this place," Joey confided. "By the time we got here, they already had him boxed up."

"So what…" Lauren wet her lips. "…what good does it do to try to get at him now?"

"Well, it's like this. Your lover boy's gonna

swear everything he told 'em was a lie, see? The boss's lawyers will have a field day if the feds try to pin anything on him without no witness to back it up.''

Lauren's heart pumped. Although she suspected she knew the answer to the question that seared into her mind, she asked it anyway.

''Why would he say he lied?''

Smiling, he took a long, lazy drag. ''You, doll. If he wants to see you alive again before he dies, he'll eat his words.''

Lauren hated him in that minute. Hated him and his pal with the same intensity as she despised the man who'd sent them out to Palm Springs.

''And if he doesn't?''

His amused smile stayed in place, but his eyes telegraphed a remorseless unconcern that sent a fresh wave of terror through her veins.

''Then you'll meet with an unfortunate accident and the boss's lawyers will have to work a little harder.''

He was enjoying this, she realized. The fat little bastard was enjoying this. Anger worked its way through her suffocating fear.

''They'll know,'' she spit out. ''If anything happens to me or to Dave, the police will know who's behind it.''

His shoulders lifted. ''As the boss says, knowing is one thing, proving is another.''

His callous attitude toward murder stopped Lauren's lungs. It was several seconds before she could speak again.

"Where is Mullvane? Why isn't he here?"

He didn't blink when she said the name. She knew then that Joey and his partner didn't intend for her to leave Palm Springs alive. Her *or* David Jannisek.

"You don't think he's gonna show his face around here with the feds swarmin' all over the place, do you? Nah, he'll sit tight in Phoenix while we finish the job them other idiots botched six weeks ago."

"What makes you think you can finish anything?" she scoffed, putting all she had into a desperate effort to keep him talking. "Dave's in federal custody. They're not going to let him just walk into a trap."

"Get real, doll. Your friend's just a little fish, and they're after the big barracudas." He tapped his shirt pocket, his eyes glinting with malicious amusement. "When we call ol' Dave and send him for a nice long drive, them cops will be crawlin' up his backside the whole way. They're gonna find a little surprise waitin' for 'em when they get where we tell 'em to go. Something that goes boom, see?"

Lauren saw. Oh, God, she saw! Dave would drive out to the appointed spot. Marsh would go with him. Or go alone, standing in for the real target, just as Lauren had stood in for Becky. He wouldn't pass up the chance to snare Mullvane, or at least snare these direct links to Mullvane.

She couldn't let these scum use her to bait another deadly trap. She had to get away. Had to warn Marsh.

Desperation pounded in her ears. The sound of her own frustration and fear drowned out everything else. Not until she'd dragged in long, steadying gulps of the chlorine-and-nicotine scented air did her thundering panic subside. She had to think! Had to stop wallowing in fear and helplessness and *do* something!

Forcing herself to look with a less-panicked eye, she searched the grotto for a sharp projection or ragged edge or even a rough spot on the marble columns, *anything* that might cut through the tape on her wrists. The pristine surroundings defeated her. She couldn't find so much as a promising rock.

Heart hammering, she stared out through the blinding sunlight to the glass doors of the sunroom. She could tell Joey she had to go to the bathroom. Maybe there was something inside the empty house she could use to cut the tape. Or—

Her gaze caught on the white latticework screen a few yards away. She could hear the hum of a motor hidden behind it. Her stomach jumped.

What had Marsh said when he showed her how to work the generator at the cabin?

Don't touch any engine parts while it's running. They get hot. Real hot.

The motor behind that screen was an engine. Maybe, just maybe it got hot, too. If she could distract Joey, even for a few minutes, and crawl over....

That desperate scheme fizzled even as it formed. Pool pump makers wouldn't manufacture products that might burn their wealthy clients.

But...

Her gaze dropped to the cigarette butt lying on the marble just inches from her foot. Its tip still glowed a faint coral.

She eyed the man slouched on the bench opposite hers through the screen of her lashes. He looked almost bored, his fingers tapping the marble table while he waited for the call that would trigger at least one, perhaps more, cold-blooded murders.

Swallowing her rage and fear, Lauren lifted her head.

"Can I have a cigarette?"

"Yeah, why not?"

He lit a fresh one from his own and placed it between her lips. She hadn't smoked since those few packs she'd experimented with in college, but she drew the tar and nicotine into her lungs like a half-drowned man would air.

Chapter 15

"Interstate Ten. Mile marker fifty-seven. I've got it."

His veins icy with fury, Marsh listened through headphones as Jannisek repeated the instructions that had just been passed to him. In the taut silence gripping the group gathered around the table, Marsh could almost hear the tension snapping along Jannisek's nerves. His own had cracked like summer lightning with the first ring of the phone. Clutching the receiver with sweat-slick fingers, the hotelier followed the instructions Marsh had drilled into him over and over.

"Let me speak to her."

The short, pithy reply roiled Marsh's stomach. Tasting bitter gall, he bit back on the response he

wanted to fling at the scum on the other end of the
line.

"Damn you," Jannisek snarled. "I'm not driving
anywhere until I talk to her and know she's okay.
Put her on!"

Marsh held his breath. So did everyone else in the
room, including, he saw in a quick sweep, Becky.
White-faced and trembling, she looked even more
frightened now than she had when she'd burst into
the suite with the news that Lauren had disappeared.

Marsh's gut twisted. It felt more like a year than
a few hours. He hadn't taken a whole breath since
a maid reported seeing an auburn-haired woman
climb into a car with two men. With only a vague
description of the vehicle to work with, Marsh had
exploded into action. In short order, he called the
resort security officer, the state highway patrol and
the local police department. He'd ordered road-
blocks set up, sent men to sweep the airport and
transformed the suite into a pulsing command post.
Despite the frenzy of activity, they'd found nothing,
heard nothing, until a few moments ago.

"Dave!"

Lauren's desperate cry almost ripped Marsh's
heart from his chest.

"I'm here," Jannisek replied swiftly.

"Don't do it! They—!"

The sound of a vicious slap was followed by a
gasp that knifed into Marsh's soul. Then the same,
smoke-roughened voice that had issued the curt instructions a moment ago repeated them.

"Mile marker fifty-seven, thirty minutes from now. You miss it by a minute, pal, and Becky here is dead."

"You hurt her again, you son of a bitch, and…"

Dave was talking to an empty line. Tight with fury, he started to slam the receiver down, but remembered just in time that he was supposed to keep the line open as long as possible.

His empty threat was still hanging in the air when Marsh tore off his headphones and spun to a third listener hunched over a metal suitcase. According to the FBI technician who'd lugged the kit in when he'd first arrived two days ago, it contained the latest high-tech electronic scanning and recording equipment. Marsh could only be thankful the FBI had brought their gear along in anticipation of unexpected contingencies like this one.

"Give me a minute," the tech muttered. "The call came from a digital cellphone. I'm trying to pinpoint the signal tower that relayed it."

A muscle jumping in the side of his jaw, Marsh strode back to the table. "Mile marker fifty-seven," he snapped to the uniformed officer who'd augmented their team. "Where is it?"

The local jabbed a finger at a spot on the topographical map spread across the table.

"Smack in the middle of the desert. They didn't give us much time. It'll take us fifteen, twenty minutes to get there. The land's as flat as roadkill along that stretch of Interstate 10," he added. "You can see for ten miles in every direction."

One of the FBI operatives exploded. "Great! We won't be able to pre-position any forces before we send in a decoy."

"We're not sending in a decoy," Jannisek said, with a shake of his head.

The flat statement wrung a cry from Becky. "Dave! No!"

"They'll be watching for a switch. I can't gamble with Lauren's life. I'm driving out there myself."

"You'll be taking along a passenger," Marsh informed him grimly. "We'll get you suited in body armor and I'll…"

"Hey! I've got it!"

The triumphant cry spun them all around. Becky's nails dug into Dave's arm as the technician tugged off his earphones. With a rustle of paper, he folded an aerial map down to single sheet size and stabbed at it with a pencil.

"The relaying tower that forwarded the call is on the east side of the city right…here."

Marsh snatched the map out of his hands. "What's the radius of signals that tower receives?"

"About three miles. I'll have to call the phone company to verify the precise number."

"Call them!"

Clutching Dave's arm, Becky crowded between him and Marsh. She hadn't changed in the tense hour since Lauren disappeared. She still wore her bathing suit and cover-up, her skin was scented with suntan lotion. She'd hardly spoken after her initial burst of near panic.

She hadn't uttered a word of blame. Hadn't thrown so much as an accusing glance Marsh's way. She didn't have to.

She could never blame him for putting Lauren in harm's way as much as he blamed himself. If anything happened to her...if he lost her now...

Grabbing a felt-tipped pen, he slashed a circle on the city map. "Three miles encompasses roughly this area."

The Palm Springs police officer leaned forward. "I know that neighborhood. It's all big estates. There aren't more than eight, ten houses inside that circle."

"Get some men out there knocking on doors. Now!"

"You got it!"

While the local snatched up the phone, the choices machine-gunned through Marsh's mind. He could go with Dave on the chance that Lauren would be staked out like a goat waiting for slaughter at mile marker fifty-seven. Or he could follow his instincts and chase down the exact location of the call.

His gut told him that the men who'd taken her wouldn't transport her to the rendezvous point. They had to know the city was swarming with cops looking for her, that choppers and snipers with high-powered scopes would converge on the area. They wanted Dave there. They'd planned something—a time-fuse bomb, pressure-sensitive plastic explosives, something!—for Jannisek. And they didn't need Lauren to make their kill.

Shooting out his wrist, Marsh checked his watch. If they were going to make the rendezvous point on time, he had one, maybe two minutes to decide. Icy sweat pooled at the base of his spine. If he chose wrong…if anything happened to Lauren before he found her…

"Are you a betting man, Henderson?"

Marsh's head jackknifed up.

"Sometimes."

"I'm thinking that the odds are they won't bring Lauren to mile marker fifty-seven."

A muscle ticked at the side of his jaw. "So am I."

Now!

She had to do it now!

Too many minutes had ticked by since that terrifying phone call. Lauren had to call Marsh. Had to stop him and Dave from taking that fatal drive.

She didn't doubt for a moment Marsh would accompany Jannisek. He'd know Mullvane or some of his henchmen had set the trap. He'd tear them apart to keep them from hurting her as they'd hurt his sister-in-law.

She had to do it now!

Her throat rasped from the noxious weeds she'd forced herself to beg from Joey. The side of her face still ached from his vicious swipe. At least the bastard had felt enough remorse to light another cigarette and place it between her shaking lips.

He was puffing away on another, too. Antsy now

that the end was near, he'd pushed off the marble bench. His back to Lauren, he ambled along the terrace, sneering at the over-sized statues of Greek gods that lined the pool. No doubt the little scum was envious of the gods' magnificent endowments, Lauren thought viciously.

It was time to implement her plan.

She swallowed a sob of laughter. She could almost see Marsh's grin when she told him how she'd planned her escape, step by step, phase by phase. Now, all she had to do was pull it off!

Her whole body tensing, she sucked in a last drag. Then slowly, so slowly, she twisted to one side and opened her lips. The filter stuck to her dry lips for terrifying seconds before it dropped to the bench beside her. Almost sobbing with relief that it hadn't bounced off the seat, she angled to one side and fumbled behind her with her bound hands.

The glowing tip grazed her fingers. She felt a stinging burn and bit down hard on her lower lip. Gently, not wanting to knock off the burning ember, she turned it end on end to grasp the filter.

The knowledge that she had only this one chance ate like acid on Lauren's nerves. Watching Joey, willing him with every fiber of her being, to keep gawking at the statues, she pressed the cigarette against the tape.

She'd never dreamed it could take so long for thin white tape to smolder—or that she wouldn't even feel the burns when it did. She sat rigid, afraid to draw attention to herself with so much as a blink, as the plastic coating on the tape caught and tiny flames licked at her arms.

Fearing Becky's pink cotton sweater might catch, too, Lauren stretched her arms as far behind her as she could. The sickening smell of burning plastic drifted up to compete with the scent of chlorine and flowering vines. Then, suddenly, her hands were free.

She had only seconds for what came next.

Bending, she ripped the tape from her ankles. Luckily, it had wrapped around her jeans more than her skin and came off easily. But not soundlessly. The snicker of the tape tearing loose sounded like cannon-fire in her ears. She froze, and threw a glance at Joey.

He hadn't heard it!

Now for Phase Two.

She couldn't think about the chances of success. Didn't dare calculate her odds. All she could do was pray her shaky legs would hold her as she launched herself off the bench, out of the grotto and across the terrace.

"What the hell…?"

Joey whirled at the exact instant Lauren barreled into him. Openmouthed with surprise, he flailed his arms madly to keep from toppling into the pool. Lauren ducked under his elbow and ripped the phone from his shirt pocket with one hand. The other she fisted and plowed as hard as she could into his flabby gut.

He didn't go down! Dear God, he didn't go down!

Off balance, spewing vile oaths, he reached across his chest for his gun. Frantic, furious, Lauren put everything she had into a huge shove. He fired one wild shot, almost deafening her, then went windmilling off the pool ledge.

He hadn't even hit water before she'd spun around and was racing for the house. She heard the splash, heard his curse end in a glub just seconds before she sent the glass doors crashing back on their slides.

With the stink of cordite and fear thick in her throat, she stabbed frantically at the phone keys as she ran. 911. She had to reach 911. They could relay a message to Marsh. Jamming the phone to her ear, she fumbled for the dead bolt on the front door, panting, praying, pleading for someone to answer.

"Hello, this is 911. What is the nature of your emergency?"

"I was kidnapped! There's going to be a murder!" She wrenched open the door. "I have to reach Special Agent Mar—ooopf!"

"Hello? Hello? Miss, are you all right?"

Stunned by her full-force collision with a wall of muscle coiled to tensile steel, Lauren reeled back. Hard hands banded her arms with brutal possession.

"Lauren! Are you all right?"

"I...I..."

"Miss! Miss!" The operator's voice leaped from the phone. "Can you answer me? Are you in imminent danger?"

Like a fool, she stuttered and sobbed and squeaked out her incredulous relief.

"Marsh! Oh, God, Marsh!"

She had one moment of blessed happiness. Three, maybe four seconds of joy. Then Marsh shoved her violently aside. She toppled off the front stoop and landed atop a shrub at the same instant shots split the air.

She was up on one knee, frantically fighting free of the bush when a horrific boom rattled the mansion's windows. Only after she'd reassured herself that Marsh still stood, whole and unbloodied, did she notice the billowing cloud of black smoke that rose out of the desert far to the west.

Chapter 16

At the sound of heavy footsteps on the scrubbed hospital tiles, Lauren looked up from the unappetizing sight of her as-yet-unbandaged left wrist. Her stomach clenched at the expression on Marsh's face.

"Is he dead?"

"No." His eyes went to her wrist. A muscle jumped in the side of his jaw. "I wanted him dead. I had my Glock sighted right in the middle of the guy's forehead."

"But you drilled a nice, neat hole right through his shoulder instead," the physician's assistant finished, grinning over his shoulder at Marsh.

"He's more use to us alive than dead," Marsh said, keeping his gaze locked on Lauren's raw, oozing wrist. The muscle in his jaw jumped again as the PA deftly twisted a light gauze bandage around the weeping flesh.

"There. We don't want to wrap them too tight. I'll give you some rolls of gauze to take with you. Spread the antiseptic cream on the burns three times a day and use a sterile wash."

"Will they scar?"

He didn't dodge Marsh's tense question. "Probably. She should consult a plastic surgeon when she gets home."

"Right now," Lauren interjected, "all she wants is one of those pain pills the doc prescribed."

Marsh was at her side in an instant. "Are you hurting?"

"Like you wouldn't believe."

She managed to toss it off lightly, but that was about all she could manage. Her hands shook when she reached for the water glass and pill the PA held out for her.

His brows slashing, Marsh took the glass and tipped it to her lips. She washed away the raspy taste of cigarette smoke and fear with a wobbly smile.

"Thanks."

"That painkiller is pretty potent," the PA warned. "You'd better sit here for a while and give it time to kick in before you step outside. Even a slight breeze on those bandages is going to sting."

Lauren suspected he'd understated the case considerably. She was more than happy to sit on the exam table for a while, particularly when Marsh stood beside her.

He looked about as whipped as she felt. The hand he'd raked through his hair while he'd waited for the doc to examine the scuzzball in the next cubicle had left it standing in dark spikes. Blood stained his blue shirt. The blood was hers, Lauren presumed, since he'd taken one look at her scorched wrists, lifted her out of the prickly shrub beside the stoop, and carried her to the black-and-white police cruiser flashing its lights in the drive. Leaving two uniformed officers to tend the wounded Joey, he'd cradled her until the ambulance arrived.

Still dazed by his arrival on the scene, deafened by the shots fired just inches from her ear and ripped apart inside by the black cloud rising out of the desert, Lauren had waited, watched and wept with frustration when the FBI agent at the scene of the explosion radioed Marsh that he'd brief him in person when he returned to Palm Springs.

"Have you heard anything?" she asked him now, her worries sharpening as the white hot needles of pain slowly dulled.

"No."

"How's Becky?"

"She's taking it hard."

Lauren bit her lip, sharing her sister's agony. If Marsh had fired a second later—if his bullet hadn't spun Joey sideways and thrown off his aim—Lauren, too, might be sitting hollow-eyed and desolate with grief.

Residual fear hiccupped through her. She ached to throw her arms around Marsh and hang on to him

for the rest of eternity. Instead, she could only hold
her wrists limply crossed and blink back tears.

"I was so afraid," she confessed.

"Me, too."

"I knew you'd figure out Mullvane was behind
my disappearance. I thought you'd go in Dave's
stead and try to snare him. All I could think about
was getting word to you that he wasn't there, and it
was a trap."

"All I could think about was *you*. I didn't care
about Mullvane. I didn't care about anything except
finding you."

He lifted a hand to brush a straggle of hair from
her cheek. His eyes reflected an aching remorse.

"I'm sorry, Lauren."

"For?"

"For dragging you into this. For letting those bas-
tards hurt you." His palm cupped her cheek. "For
not telling you that I love you."

She cocked her head and blinked up at him. "The
painkiller must have kicked into high gear. I'm getting woozy. I could have sworn you said you love
me."

"I did."

His thumb did that lip thing again, that slow, mad-
dening stroke that had driven Lauren crazy last
night. Or was it the night before? She couldn't seem
to remember. She caught that marauding thumb in
a kiss.

The awful remorse left his eyes, giving way to a
rueful glint.

"I was kind of hoping you weren't too woozy to respond in kind."

"I'm not." Her smile shook around the edges, but it came from her heart. "And I do. Love you, I mean. Desperately. Passionately. With all my heart and soul and everything. I will even," she announced with a lopsided grin, "buy some white-lace thong panties to wear under my wedding dress."

Marsh's face lit with laughter.

"You will, huh? Then I guess we'd better hit the shops as soon as we blow this place."

"But…" She shook her head in a futile attempt to clear the fuzzies. "…but what about Mullvane? Don't you have to go, you know, do your special agent thing?"

"Mullvane can wait. You, my darling Lauren, can't."

Epilogue

Marsh stood behind Lauren, shielding her from the December wind that howled down from the San Franciscos and whipped the light dusting of snow into a thousand tiny whirlwinds. The collar of his sheepskin jacket protected his ears. His pulled-down dress black Stetson sat low on his forehead to resist the wind's tug.

They'd come home to the Bar-H, he and Lauren. Becky had come with them, along with the sisters' divorced parents, their aunt Jane and Lauren's assistant, Josh, all assembled for a belated celebration of the marriage that had taken them all by surprise.

The Hendersons had all gathered, too. Sam and Molly and Kasey. Reece and Sydney. Evan, wheeling his Harley through the snow that had dropped out of the skies without warning and cursing every mile. Marsh's mother, Jessica, her dove-gray hair short and sassy and her smile aglow for her newest daughter-in-law.

Jake had shaken off his grief to welcome them. Even Shad had appeared, all decked out in his best shirt and offering to squire a blushing Aunt Jane on a tour of the barns and stables.

They were waiting back at the house. All of them.

But Lauren had wanted this moment alone with Marsh. Her hair whipping around her face, she bent to place a bouquet of winter roses on Ellen's grave. The wind caught her sigh as she straightened and leaned against her husband. His arms came around her.

"I wish I'd known her."

"You would have liked her."

They stood quietly for a moment. Idly, Lauren lifted a hand to tuck the tossing strands of red behind her ear. Marsh's stomach knotted when he glimpsed the stretch of puckered skin between her sleeve and her glove.

"I'm glad you took Mullvane down."

"So am I," he said fiercely.

Even after all these weeks, he couldn't quite believe how easy it had been. Faced with kidnapping and attempted murder charges, Joey had spilled his guts. Within hours, they'd put together enough to convince a judge to issue warrants. Within days, they'd led the protesting, sputtering Mullvane away in handcuffs. Between the two events, Lauren had comforted her grief-stricken sister and fulfilled her promise to wear a pair of white-lace thong panties under her ivory satin wedding suit. Marsh still shivered whenever he remembered their wedding night.

Now they'd come home.

And now, with Mullvane's trial only weeks away, Marsh had to tell his wife what he couldn't tell her before. His hands gentle on her waist, he turned her in his arms.

"Lauren, Dave Jannisek didn't die in the explosion."

"What!"

"When we pulled up the drive of that vacant house and I heard the shot, I knew in my gut I'd found you. I had the driver of the cruiser get on the radio. He contacted Dave while I was racing to the house."

"What!"

"Jannisek bailed out of his car just short of the detonation point."

Stunned, Lauren gaped up at him. Joy waged a fierce battle with outrage, taking her face from white with cold to an angry red.

"He was injured by the flying debris," Marsh told her. "For weeks, we weren't sure he was going to make it."

Remembering his first view of the gaping hole that was once a four-lane interstate, he marveled that Jannisek had survived at all. The murderers who'd tried to take him out had used almost as much explosive as the terrorists who'd blown up the World Trade Center.

"And you didn't tell Becky! Or me!"

"I wanted to, but Dave swore me to silence. He didn't want..." He stopped and corrected himself. "He *doesn't* want to put her in danger again. Until the trial's over and he disappears for good, there's still the chance Mullvane will try to take him out."

That stopped Lauren's river of protests. Her jaw shut with a snap. She'd think about that, Marsh knew. Weigh all the ramifications before letting loose with both barrels. Right now her main concern was her sister.

"Can we tell Becky?"

"Only if she agrees not to contact Dave in any way before or after the trial."

"But..."

"Those are his conditions, not mine."

She didn't like that. Eyes stormy, she scowled at Marsh as though it was his fault Becky had cried herself to sleep these past weeks.

That's what he loved most about this woman who was now his wife. Her fierce loyalty to her sister, and, more recently, to Marsh and his family. She didn't put limits on her love, which both humbled him and filled him in ways he'd never imagined. He'd never get enough of it—or of her.

"Do you want to know the kicker?" he asked, his arms and his heart full.

"I'm not sure I can take any more right now."

"Because of Mullvane's connections in Phoenix,

his trial's been moved to Southern California. Evan's one of the prosecuting attorneys.''

"Evan!'' She blinked the snow off her lashes. ''Isn't that a conflict of interest or something?''

"Actually,'' he replied, with the beginnings of a grin, ''Evan sees it as a reprieve. Now that I'm out of the picture, Reece's wife, Sydney, has turned her matchmaking eye on him. He needs a long, complicated trial like this to keep him occupied and her off his case. He can't convince her he's not ready for marriage.''

Putting her shock and anger aside for the moment, she leaned back in his arms.

"Too bad,'' she murmured, brushing the snow from his cheeks with a fingertip. ''Evan doesn't know what he's missing.''

"He'll find out one of these days. Just as I did.''

Bending down, he brushed her lips with his. Wintery warm and petal soft, they welcomed him in from the cold.

*   *   *   *   *

THOSE MARRYING McBRIDES!:

The four *single* McBride siblings have always been
unlucky in love. But it looks as if their luck is
about to change....

Rancher Joe McBride was a man who'd sworn off big-city
women. But his vow was about to be sorely tested when
he met Angel Wiley. Don't miss A RANCHING MAN
(IM #992), Linda Turner's next installment in her
Those Marrying McBrides! miniseries—
on sale in March 2000

And coming in June 2000, *Those Marrying McBrides!*
continues with Merry's story in
THE BEST MAN (IM #1010).
Available at your favorite retail outlet.

To order, send the completed form, along with a check or money order for the total
above, payable to Silhouette Books, to: **In the U.S.:** 3010 Walden Avenue, P.O. Box 9077,
Buffalo, NY 14269-9077; **In Canada:** P.O. Box 636, Fort Erie, Ontario, L2A 5X3.

Name: _____

Address: _____ City: _____

State/Prov.: _____ Zip/Postal Code: _____

Account # (if applicable): _____   075 CSAS

*New York residents remit applicable sales taxes.
 Canadian residents remit applicable
 GST and provincial taxes.

Visit us at www.romance.net
SIMMCB

Where love comes alive™

Looking For More Romance?

Visit Romance.net

Look us up on-line at: http://www.romance.net

Check in daily for these and other exciting features:

Hot off the press

View all current titles, and purchase them on-line.

What do the stars have in store for you?

Horoscope

Hot deals

Exclusive offers available only at Romance.net

Plus, don't miss our interactive quizzes, contests and bonus gifts.

PWEB

SUZANNE BROCKMANN

continues her popular,
heart-stopping miniseries

*They're who you call to get you out of
a tight spot—or into one!*

Coming in November 1999
THE ADMIRAL'S BRIDE, IM #962

Be sure to catch Mitch's story,
IDENTITY: UNKNOWN, IM #974,
in January 2000.

And **Lucky's story** in April 2000.

And in December 1999 be sure to pick up a
copy of Suzanne's powerful installment
in the **Royally Wed** miniseries,
UNDERCOVER PRINCESS, IM #968.

Available at your favorite retail outlet.

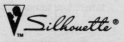

Visit us at www.romance.net

SIMTDD2

Celebrate the joy of bringing a baby into the world—
and the power of passionate love—with

A BOUQUET OF BABIES

An anthology containing three delightful stories
from three beloved authors!

THE WAY HOME
The classic tale from *New York Times* bestselling author

LINDA
HOWARD

FAMILY BY FATE
A brand-new Maternity Row story by
PAULA DETMER RIGGS

BABY ON HER DOORSTEP
A brand-new Twins on the Doorstep story by
STELLA BAGWELL

Available in April 2000, at your favorite retail outlet.

Silhouette®
Where love comes alive™

Visit us at www.romance.net   PSBOUQ

INTIMATE MOMENTS®

Silhouette®

INVITES YOU TO CELEBRATE THE
PUBLICATION OF OUR

1000TH BOOK!

And to mark the occasion, award-winning author

MAGGIE SHAYNE

brings you another installment of

Look for

ANGEL MEETS THE BADMAN

on sale April 2000 at your favorite retail outlet.

*And don't forget to order copies of the first six tales
about the irresistible Brands:*

THE LITTLEST COWBOY, IM #716 (6/96) $3.99 U.S./$4.50 CAN.
THE BADDEST VIRGIN IN TEXAS, IM #788(6/97) $3.99 U.S./$4.50 CAN.
BADLANDS BAD BOY, IM #809 (9/97) $3.99 U.S./$4.50 CAN.
THE HUSBAND SHE COULDN'T REMEMBER, IM #854 (5/98) $4.25 U.S./$4.75 CAN.
THE BADDEST BRIDE IN TEXAS, IM #907 (2/99) $4.25 U.S./$4.75 CAN.
THE OUTLAW BRIDE, IM #967 (12/99) $4.25 U.S./$4.75 CAN.

To order, send the completed form, along with a check or money order for the total
above, payable to Silhouette Books, to: **In the U.S.:** 3010 Walden Avenue, P.O. Box 9077,
Buffalo, NY 14269-9077; **In Canada:** P.O. Box 636, Fort Erie, Ontario, L2A 5X3.

Name: _____

Address: _____ City: _____

State/Prov.: _____ Zip/Postal Code: _____

Account # (if applicable): _____ 075 CSAS

*New York residents remit applicable sales taxes.
Canadian residents remit applicable
GST and provincial taxes.

Visit us at www.romance.net
SIMTB1

Silhouette®

Where love comes alive™

THE FORTUNES OF TEXAS

Membership in this family has its privileges…and its price. But what a fortune can't buy, a true-bred Texas love is sure to bring!

On sale in March…

The Heiress and the Sheriff

by **STELLA BAGWELL**

Sheriff Wyatt Grayhawk didn't trust strangers, especially the lovely damsel who claimed to have no memory yet sought a haven on the Fortunes' Texas ranch. But would Wyatt's mission to uncover Gabrielle's past be sidetracked by the allure of the mysterious beauty?

THE FORTUNES OF TEXAS continues with **LONE STAR WEDDING**

by Sandra Steffen, available in April from Silhouette Books.

Available at your favorite retail outlet.

Silhouette®

Where love comes alive™

Visit us at www.romance.net

PSFOT8

SILHOUETTE'S 20ᵀᴴ ANNIVERSARY CONTEST
OFFICIAL RULES
NO PURCHASE NECESSARY TO ENTER

1. To enter, follow directions published in the offer to which you are responding. Contest begins 1/1/00 and ends on 8/24/00 (the "Promotion Period"). Method of entry may vary. Mailed entries must be postmarked by 8/24/00, and received by 8/31/00.

2. During the Promotion Period, the Contest may be presented via the Internet. Entry via the Internet may be restricted to residents of certain geographic areas that are disclosed on the Web site. To enter via the Internet, if you are a resident of a geographic area in which Internet entry is permissible, follow the directions displayed on-line, including typing your essay of 100 words or fewer telling us "Where In The World Your Love Will Come Alive." On-line entries must be received by 11:59 p.m. Eastern Standard time on 8/24/00. Limit one e-mail entry per person, household and e-mail address per day, per presentation. If you are a resident of a geographic area in which entry via the Internet is permissible, you may, in lieu of submitting an entry on-line, enter by mail, by hand-printing your name, address, telephone number and contest number/name on an 8"x 11" plain piece of paper and telling us in 100 words or fewer "Where In The World Your Love Will Come Alive," and mailing via first-class mail to: Silhouette 20ᵗʰ Anniversary Contest, (in the U.S.) P.O. Box 9069, Buffalo, NY 14269-9069; (In Canada) P.O. Box 637, Fort Erie, Ontario, Canada L2A 5X3. Limit one 8"x 11" mailed entry per person, household and e-mail address per day. On-line and/or 8"x 11" mailed entries received from persons residing in geographic areas in which Internet entry is not permissible will be disqualified. No liability is assumed for lost, late, incomplete, inaccurate, nondelivered or misdirected mail, or misdirected e-mail, for technical, hardware or software failures of any kind, lost or unavailable network connection, or failed, incomplete, garbled or delayed computer transmission or any human error which may occur in the receipt or processing of the entries in the contest.

3. Essays will be judged by a panel of members of the Silhouette editorial and marketing staff based on the following criteria:

>   Sincerity (believability, credibility)—50%
>   Originality (freshness, creativity)—30%
>   Aptness (appropriateness to contest ideas)—20%

Purchase or acceptance of a product offer does not improve your chances of winning. In the event of a tie, duplicate prizes will be awarded.

4. All entries become the property of Harlequin Enterprises Ltd., and will not be returned. Winner will be determined no later than 10/31/00 and will be notified by mail. Grand Prize winner will be required to sign and return Affidavit of Eligibility within 15 days of receipt of notification. Noncompliance within the time period may result in disqualification and an alternative winner may be selected. All municipal, provincial, federal, state and local laws and regulations apply. Contest open only to residents of the U.S. and Canada who are 18 years of age or older, and is void wherever prohibited by law. Internet entry is restricted solely to residents of those geographical areas in which Internet entry is permissible. Employees of Torstar Corp., their affiliates, agents and members of their immediate families are not eligible. Taxes on the prizes are the sole responsibility of winners. Entry and acceptance of any prize offered constitutes permission to use winner's name, photograph or other likeness for the purposes of advertising, trade and promotion on behalf of Torstar Corp. without further compensation to the winner, unless prohibited by law. Torstar Corp and D.L. Blair, Inc., their parents, affiliates and subsidiaries, are not responsible for errors in printing or electronic presentation of contest or entries. In the event of printing or other errors which may result in unintended prize values or duplication of prizes, all affected contest materials or entries shall be null and void. If for any reason the Internet portion of the contest is not capable of running as planned, including infection by computer virus, bugs, tampering, unauthorized intervention, fraud, technical failures, or any other causes beyond the control of Torstar Corp. which corrupt or affect the administration, secrecy, fairness, integrity or proper conduct of the contest, Torstar Corp. reserves the right, at its sole discretion, to disqualify any individual who tampers with the entry process and to cancel, terminate, modify or suspend the contest or the Internet portion thereof. In the event of a dispute regarding an on-line entry, the entry will be deemed submitted by the authorized holder of the e-mail account submitted at the time of entry. Authorized account holder is defined as the natural person who is assigned to an e-mail address by an Internet access provider, on-line service provider or other organization that is responsible for arranging e-mail address for the domain associated with the submitted e-mail address.

5. Prizes: Grand Prize—a $10,000 vacation to anywhere in the world. Travelers (at least one must be 18 years of age or older) or parent or guardian if one traveler is a minor, must sign and return a Release of Liability prior to departure. Travel must be completed by December 31, 2001, and is subject to space and accommodations availability. Two hundred (200) Second Prizes—a two-book limited edition autographed collector set from one of the Silhouette Anniversary authors: Nora Roberts, Diana Palmer, Linda Howard or Annette Broadrick (value $10.00 each set). All prizes are valued in U.S. dollars.

6. For a list of winners (available after 10/31/00), send a self-addressed, stamped envelope to: Harlequin Silhouette 20ᵗʰ Anniversary Winners, P.O. Box 4200, Blair, NE 68009-4200.

Contest sponsored by Torstar Corp., P.O. Box 9042, Buffalo, NY 14269-9042.

ENTER FOR
A CHANCE TO WIN*

Silhouette's 20th Anniversary Contest

Tell Us Where in the World
You Would Like *Your* Love To Come Alive...
And We'll Send the Lucky Winner There!

Silhouette wants to take you wherever
your happy ending can come true.

Here's how to enter: Tell us, in 100 words or less,
where you want to go to make your love come alive!

In addition to the grand prize, there will be 200
runner-up prizes, collector's-edition book sets
autographed by one of the Silhouette anniversary
authors: **Nora Roberts, Diana Palmer,
Linda Howard** or **Annette Broadrick**.

DON'T MISS YOUR CHANCE TO WIN!
ENTER NOW! No Purchase Necessary

Silhouette®
TM   *Where love comes alive*™

Name:

Address:

City: State/Province:

Zip/Postal Code:

Mail to Harlequin Books: **In the U.S.:** P.O. Box 9069, Buffalo, NY
14269-9069; **In Canada:** P.O. Box 637, Fort Erie, Ontario, L4A 5X3

*No purchase necessary—for contest details send a self-addressed stamped envelope to:
Silhouette's 20th Anniversary Contest, P.O. Box 9069, Buffalo, NY, 14269-9069 (include
contest name on self-addressed envelope). Residents of Washington and Vermont may
omit postage. Open to Cdn. (excluding Quebec) and U.S. residents who are 18 or over.
Void where prohibited. Contest ends August 31, 2000.

PS20CON_R